KALOS ESSENTIAL ACTIVITY BOOK

SCHOLASTIC INC.

KALOS ESSENTIAL ACTIVITY BOOK

SCHOLASTIC INC.

ISBN 978-0-545-92749-9

10 9 8 7 6 5 4 3 2 1 16 17 18 19 20

Printed in Malaysia 106

First printing 2016

CONTENTS

POKéMON
TM

THE ADVENTURE CONTINUES . . .

GOOD-BYE, UNOVA, WELCOME TO KALOS!

Some time ago, daring young Trainer Ash Ketchum started on the path toward becoming a Pokémon Master in Pallet Town in the Kanto region. Now he and his loyal buddy Pikachu continue their journey in the beautiful Kalos region. So far their travels have taken them on an exciting quest through the incredible regions of Kanto, Johto, Hoenn, Sinnoh, and Unova.

Ash has learned a lot about Pokémon behavior, and he is constantly perfecting his craft, taking every opportunity to train and brush up on his battle moves and Pokémon knowledge. With an awesome collection of Gym Badges to his name, Ash is more determined than ever to pursue his dream of becoming a Pokémon Master and to show the world what he can do!

The Kalos region has a vast and varied landscape that includes rivers, mountains, caves, coastal cliffs and coves, beaches, marshlands, and forests. The region is divided into three distinct areas—Central, Coastal, and Mountain—each with its own unique geography and Pokémon. There are many towns and cities dotted throughout the region. One of the biggest towns, Lumiose City, is a busy metropolis located in the heart of the Kalos region at the point where all three areas meet.

DID YOU KNOW? The Lumiose City Gym is located in the Prism Tower.

DID YOU KNOW? Professor Sycamore's Research Lab is located in Lumiose City.

NEW FIRST PARTNER POKÉMON

In Kalos, each Trainer must choose from one of these three Pokémon: Chespin, Fennekin, or Froakie.

ASH KETCHUM'S KALOS ADVENTURE!

A confident and more experienced Ash arrives in Lumiose City, ready to explore Kalos in pursuit of the knowledge that will help him become a Pokémon Master. He has his sights set on the Kalos League and is ready to battle and catch as many new Pokémon as possible.

Before he can take on the ultimate challenge, Ash must face the formidable Gym Leaders of Kalos. Ash's Kalos adventures will lead him to many exciting discoveries, information about Pokémon Evolution, and the secrets of Mega Evolution! Pikachu will be by Ash's side throughout his journey, as well as Ash's group of traveling companions—his new friends Clemont, Serena, and Bonnie. Kalos, here they come!

FROAKIE

This Water-type Pokémon chooses Ash as its Trainer and becomes his Kalos first partner Pokémon. The foamy bubbles, or frubbles, that cover Froakie's body protect its sensitive skin from damage. It's always alert to any changes in its environment.

FLETCHLING

Fletchling is a Normal-and-Flying-type Pokémon. The Tiny Robin is the first Pokémon Ash catches in Kalos. If an intruder threatens a Fletchling's territory, it will defend it fiercely. Fletchling has a beautiful voice.

PIKACHU POWER!

This smart, feisty, and fun-loving Pokémon is Ash's best pal. When they first met, there were sparks between the headstrong pair, but over time they have learned to appreciate each other's good qualities. They have a bond and trust that's second to none. Together, Ash and Pikachu can overcome any obstacle.

Since he is so rare and highly coveted, Pikachu is vulnerable to attack and kidnap attempts, but Ash will do anything to protect his best friend. In turn, Pikachu will protect Ash at any cost.

Pikachu always rides on Ash's shoulder—he refuses to travel by the usual Poké Ball method of transport! He is the only one of Ash's Pokémon that doesn't have to use the Poké Ball.

PIKACHU PROFILE:

Mouse Pokémon

This forest-dwelling Pokémon stores electricity in its cheek pouches.

Type: Electric

Height: 1′ 04″

Weight: 13.2 lbs.

Pichu Pikachu Raichu

Possible Moves:

Growl, Thunder Shock, Tail Whip, Thunder Wave, Quick Attack, Electro Ball, Double Team, Slam, Thunderbolt, Feint, Agility, Discharge, Light Screen, Thunder, Play Nice, Nuzzle

Meet the new Pokémon TRAVELING PALS!

At the start of his Kalos adventure, Ash arrives by plane in Lumiose City with his journalist friend Alexa, who works for the *Lumiose Press*. Her sister, Viola, is a Gym Leader in Santalune City. Ash wants to challenge her, but she's away. Alexa gives Ash a map and suggests he visits the Lumiose City Gym first. That's where he meets Clemont and Bonnie, who soon become close, loyal friends, ready to join Ash in battle and on his journey through Kalos.

SERENA

When Ash meets Serena in Santalune City, they discover that they have actually met before—several years earlier at a Pokémon Summer Camp. They soon become fast friends again. Serena's mother is a world-famous Rhyhorn racer, and Serena has been training to follow in her mother's footsteps. However, Serena isn't very enthusiastic about the sport, and so, after choosing her first Partner Pokémon and becoming a young Trainer herself, she decides to join Ash, Clemont, and Bonnie on their journey through Kalos.

DEDENNE

Clemont is keeping this Electric- and Fairy-type Pokémon for his sister until she's old enough to become a Trainer herself. Dedenne uses its whiskers like antennas to communicate over long distances with electrical waves. It can soak up electricity through its tail.

BONNIE

Bonnie is Clemont's impulsive younger sister. She looks up to her big brother and loves helping him take care of his Pokémon, but is too young to have her own Pokémon yet—a fact that she doesn't like at all, although it doesn't stop her from joining Clemont and Ash on their adventures in Kalos.

FENNEKIN

This Fire-type Fox Pokémon is Serena's first partner. It is always eager to test its battling skills. Searing heat radiates from its large ears to keep opponents at a distance. It often snacks on twigs to gain energy.

CLEMONT

The shy and reserved Clemont is a bit of a genius inventor (although not all his inventions work out as planned!) as well as a Pokémon Trainer. He loves all things electronic, and is happiest when he's using his keen intellect or unique and unusual inventions to help his friends. Although Ash doesn't realize it at first, Clemont is the Lumiose City Gym Leader.

CHESPIN

This Grass-type Pokémon is Clemont's first partner. When Chespin flexes its soft quills, they become tough spikes with sharp piercing points. It relies on its nutlike shell for protection in battle.

BUNNELBY

The Normal-type Bunnelby is Clemont's go-to Pokémon for battling. It can use its ears like shovels to dig holes in the ground.

THE BAD GUYS

TEAM ROCKET

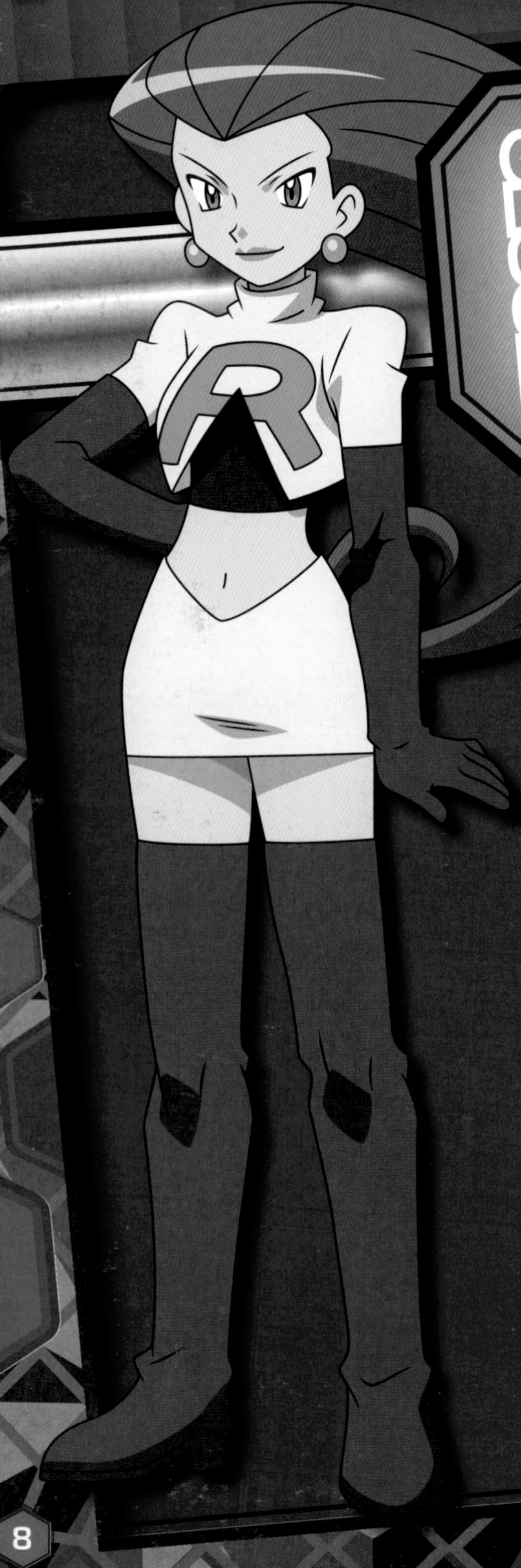

JESSIE

Appointed leader of the team, this purple-haired villain is vain, argumentative, short-tempered, and sharp-tongued. She is too tough to show her feelings or admit that she needs her teammates, and she hates weakness in others. Unfortunately for her, Jessie is not a patient Pokémon Trainer, so her attempts to snatch these valuable creatures often backfire.

WOBBUFFET

This Psychic-type Pokémon is always ready for action with Team Rocket. Although it normally avoids battle , preferring to hide in dark places, if another Pokémon attacks it first, it puffs up its body and strikes back.

You have to hand it to them—the terrible trio of Jessie, James, and Meowth doesn't ever give up. However hard Ash and Pikachu try to get away from them, Team Rocket are never far behind, ready to cause mischief and mayhem. Their schemes may be increasingly desperate and ridiculous, but they do stick to their mission, which is to try to capture Ash's Pikachu. Luckily for Ash and his friends, Team Rocket fail more than they succeed; their cluelessness usually ends up causing more trouble for themselves than for Ash!

Team Rocket work for a criminal organization run by the mysterious and evil crime lord, Giovanni. Their job is to steal valuable Pokémon, and they'd do anything to try and impress their boss. Will they succeed in capturing Pikachu and taking over the Kalos region?

Watch out, Ash . . .

They're (ALWAYS!) behind you!

MEOWTH

This talented talking Pokémon might only be a Normal-type, but he is definitely one of a criminal kind. Meowth taught himself to speak like a human and to walk on two legs. And, boy, does he know how to talk the talk! He loves nothing better than plotting evil schemes, the crazier the better. He can be very persuasive, but fortunately for Ash and his friends, most of Meowth's criminal plans go spectacularly wrong!

JAMES

Don't be fooled by this floppy-haired boy's sentimental love for his own Pokémon. He's mean and sly and is always happy to snatch and sell innocent Pokémon to make a quick buck, which makes it surprising that he left his wealthy family to lead a life of crime and intrigue.

This book contains a fact- and stat-filled list of Pokémon from the Kalos region. The Kalos Pokémon can be divided into three groups according to the different subregions of Kalos that they come from—Central, Coastal, and Mountain.

Use this Pokédex to brush up on your Pokémon knowledge! Each Pokémon is listed within its subregion for quick and easy reference. Be prepared to be amazed by these fascinating new species!

There are eighteen different Pokémon types. Dual-type Pokémon are listed under their first type. Look out for the new Fairy-type found in the Kalos region!

BUNNELBY
NORMAL

FENNEKIN
FIRE

FROAKIE
WATER

CHESPIN
GRASS

DEDENNE
ELECTRIC

CUBCHOO
ICE

MIENFOO
FIGHTING

STUNKY
POISON

GOLETT
GROUND

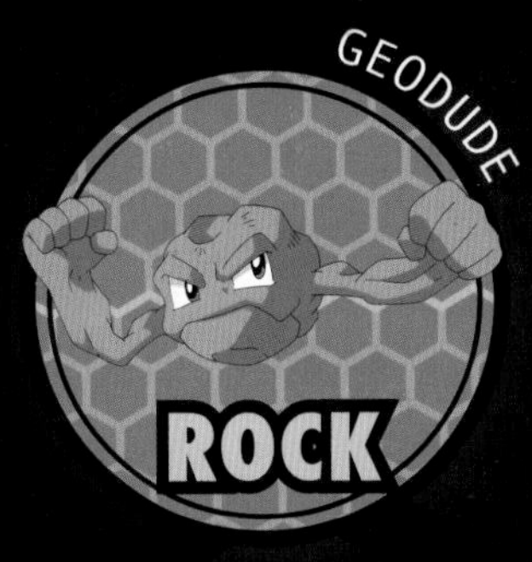

Ash discovers a new type of highly evolved Pokémon in Kalos. These Mega-Evolved Pokémon can only evolve in battle. Once the battle ends, the Mega-Evolved Pokémon will return to their usual state.

Ancient stories from each region tell of the Legendary and Mythical Pokémon. These two special groups of Pokémon are very powerful and very difficult to catch. Look in your Pokédex to check out the Legendary species unique to Kalos (Xerneas, Yveltal, Zygarde). They are tricky to find—keep a close lookout!

CHESPIN

Type: Grass
Height: 1' 04"
Weight: 19.8 lbs.

When Chespin flexes its soft quills, they become tough spikes with sharp, piercing points. It relies on its nutlike shell for protection in battle.

QUILLADIN

Type: Grass
Height: 2' 04"
Weight: 63.9 lbs.

Quilladin often train for battle by charging forcefully into one another. Despite their spiky appearance, they have a gentle nature and don't like confrontation.

CHESNAUGHT

Type: Grass-Fighting
Height: 5' 03"
Weight: 198.4 lbs.

When its friends are in trouble, Chesnaught uses its own body as a shield. Its shell is tough enough to protect it from a powerful explosion.

FENNEKIN

Type: Fire
Height: 1' 04"
Weight: 20.7 lbs.

Searing heat radiates from Fennekin's large ears to keep opponents at a distance. It often snacks on twigs to gain energy.

BRAIXEN

Type: Fire
Height: 3' 03"
Weight: 32.0 lbs.

When Braixen pulls the twig out of its tail, the friction from its fur sets the wood on fire. It can use this flaming twig as a tool or a weapon.

DELPHOX

Type: Fire-Psychic
Height: 4' 11"
Weight: 86.0 lbs.

The mystical Delphox uses a flaming branch as a focus for its psychic visions. When it gazes into the fire, it can see the future.

FROAKIE

Type: Water
Height: 1' 00"
Weight: 15.4 lbs.

The foamy bubbles that cover Froakie's body protect its sensitive skin from damage. It's always alert to any changes in its environment.

FROGADIER

Type: Water
Height: 2' 00"
Weight: 24.0 lbs.

Swift and sure, Frogadier coats pebbles in a bubbly foam and then flings them with pinpoint accuracy. It has spectacular jumping and climbing skills.

GRENINJA

Type: Water-Dark
Height: 4' 11"
Weight: 88.2 lbs.

Greninja can compress water into sharp-edged throwing stars. With the grace of a ninja, it slips in and out of sight to attack from the shadows.

BUNNELBY

Type: Normal
Height: 1' 04"
Weight: 11.0 lbs.

Bunnelby can use its ears like shovels to dig holes in the ground. Eventually, its ears become strong enough to cut through thick tree roots while it digs.

DIGGERSBY

Type: Normal-Ground
Height: 3' 03"
Weight: 93.5 lbs.

Diggersby can use their ears like excavators to move heavy boulders. Construction workers like having them around.

ZIGZAGOON

Type: Normal
Height: 1' 04"
Weight: 38.6 lbs.

The curious and easily distracted Zigzagoon walks in a distinctive zigzag pattern because it's always dashing off to check out any item it spots in the grass.

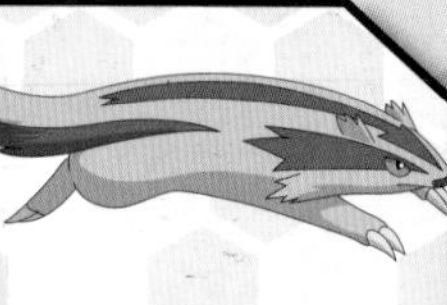

LINOONE

Type: Normal
Height: 1' 08"
Weight: 71.6 lbs.

Although it can run faster than 60 miles an hour in a straight line, Linoone often has trouble navigating curves.

FLETCHLING

Type: Normal-Flying
Height: 1' 00"
Weight: 3.7 lbs.

Flocks of Fletchling sing to one another in beautiful voices to communicate. If an intruder threatens their territory, they will defend it fiercely.

FLETCHINDER

Type: Fire-Flying
Height: 2' 04"
Weight: 35.3 lbs.

As the flame sac on Fletchinder's belly slowly heats up, it flies faster and faster. It produces embers from its beak.

TALONFLAME

Type: Fire-Flying
Height: 3' 11"
Weight: 54.0 lbs.

Talonflame can swoop at incredible speeds when attacking. During intense battles, its wings give off showers of embers as it flies.

PIDGEY

Type: Normal-Flying
Height: 1' 00"
Weight: 4.0 lbs.

Pidgey usually prefer not to fight unless they're disturbed. They stir up clouds of sand with their wings to make it harder for opponents to see them.

PIDGEOTTO

Type: Normal-Flying
Height: 3' 07"
Weight: 66.1 lbs.

The territorial Pidgeotto goes after intruders with fierce blows of its beak. Its well-developed claws can hang onto an object over many miles of flight.

PIDGEOT

Type: Normal-Flying
Height: 4' 11"
Weight: 87.1 lbs.

When in search of food, Pidgeot often swoop low over bodies of water, almost skimming the surface. They can fly faster than the speed of sound.

SCATTERBUG

Type: Bug
Height: 1' 00"
Weight: 5.5 lbs.

When threatened, Scatterbug protects itself with a cloud of black powder that can paralyze its attacker. This powder also serves as protection from the elements.

SPEWPA

Type: Bug
Height: 1' 00"
Weight: 18.5 lbs.

Like Scatterbug, Spewpa releases a protective cloud of powder when attacked. It can also bristle up its thick fur in an attempt to scare off any aggressors.

VIVILLON

Type: Bug-Flying
Height: 3' 11"
Weight: 37.5 lbs.

The colorful patterns on Vivillon's wings are determined by the Pokémon's habitat. Vivillon from different parts of the world have different wing patterns.

CATERPIE

Type: Bug
Height: 1' 00"
Weight: 6.4 lbs.

Caterpie's red antennas can produce a terrible smell to repel attackers. Its suction-cup feet stick to any surface, so it can climb high into the trees for food.

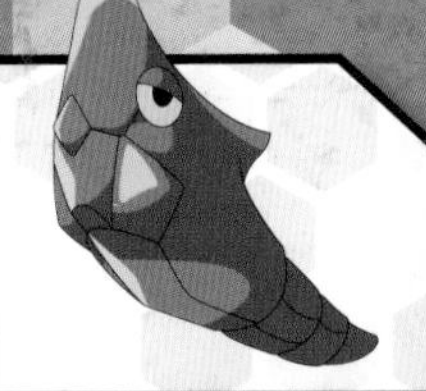

METAPOD

Type: Bug
Height: 2' 04"
Weight: 21.8 lbs.

While Metapod waits to evolve, its soft body is protected by a shell as hard as iron. The shell guards it from attacks and harsh conditions.

BUTTERFREE

Type: Bug-Flying
Height: 3' 07"
Weight: 70.5 lbs.

The dust on its wings repels water, so Butterfree has no problems flying in the rain. It seeks out flowers for their tasty nectar.

WEEDLE

Type: Bug-Poison
Height: 1' 00"
Weight: 7.1 lbs.

The two-inch barb on top of Weedle's head is a powerful poisonous stinger. It lives in wooded areas or open fields.

KAKUNA

Type: Bug-Poison
Height: 2' 00"
Weight: 22.0 lbs.

Inside its shell, Kakuna is almost immobile, so it hides in the trees. When in danger, it can make the shell harder to protect itself.

BEEDRILL

Type: Bug-Poison
Height: 3' 03"
Weight: 65.0 lbs.

Beedrill wields its three stingers viciously, jabbing at an opponent with their poisoned tips. Sometimes a group of Beedrill will swarm a single enemy.

PANSAGE

Type: Grass
Height: 2' 00"
Weight: 23.1 lbs.

Chewing the leaf from Pansage's head is a known method of stress relief. It willingly shares its leaf—along with any berries it's collected—with those who need it.

SIMISAGE

Type: Grass
Height: 3' 07"
Weight: 67.2 lbs.

Simisage's tail is covered in thorns, and it uses the tail like a whip to lash out at opponents. It always seems to be in a bad mood.

PANSEAR

Type: Fire
Height: 2' 00"
Weight: 24.3 lbs.

Clever and helpful, Pansear prefers to cook its berries rather than eating them raw. Its natural habitat is volcanic caves, so it's no surprise that its fiery tuft burns at 600 degrees Fahrenheit.

SIMISEAR

Type: Fire
Height: 3' 03"
Weight: 61.7 lbs.

Simisear's head and tail give off embers in the heat of battle . . . or anytime it's excited. It has quite a sweet tooth.

PANPOUR

Type: Water
Height: 2' 00"
Weight: 29.8 lbs.

Panpour's head tuft is full of nutrient-rich water. It uses its tail to water plants, which then grow big and healthy.

SIMIPOUR

Type: Water
Height: 3' 03"
Weight: 63.9 lbs.

Simipour can shoot water out of its tail with such force that it can punch right through a concrete wall. When its stores run low, it dips its tail into clean water to suck up a refill.

PICHU

Type: Electric
Height: 1' 00"
Weight: 4.4 lbs.

Pichu often play with each other by touching their tails together, creating a shower of electric sparks. They lack control over their own electricity and sometimes give off unexpected jolts.

PIKACHU

Type: Electric
Height: 1' 04"
Weight: 13.2 lbs.

When threatened, Pikachu can deliver a powerful zap from the electric pouches on its cheeks. Its jagged tail sometimes attracts lightning during a storm.

RAICHU

Type: Electric
Height: 2' 07"
Weight: 66.1 lbs.

Raichu can take down much larger foes with high-voltage bursts of electricity. It gets twitchy and aggressive if its electricity is allowed to build up without release.

BIDOOF

Type: Normal
Height: 1' 08"
Weight: 44.1 lbs.

Bidoof live beside the water, where they gnaw on rock or wood to keep their front teeth worn down. They have a steady nature and are not easily upset.

BIBAREL

Type: Normal-Water
Height: 3' 03"
Weight: 69.4 lbs.

With their large, sharp teeth, Bibarel busily cut up trees to build nests. Sometimes these nests block small streams and divert the flow of the water.

DUNSPARCE

Type: Normal
Height: 4' 11"
Weight: 30.9 lbs.

To escape from an enemy, Dunsparce digs frantically with its tail to burrow backward into the ground. Its subterranean nest resembles a maze.

AZURILL

Type: Normal-Fairy
Height: 0' 08"
Weight: 4.4 lbs.

When fighting off a large attacker, Azurill swings its bulbous tail around like a weight. It can also bounce on its tail to get around on land.

MARILL

Type: Water-Fairy
Height: 1' 04"
Weight: 18.7 lbs.

Marill's water-repelling fur keeps it dry even when it's playing in rivers and streams. Its buoyant tail lets it float with ease.

AZUMARILL

Type: Water-Fairy
Height: 2' 07"
Weight: 62.8 lbs.

With its long ears, Azumarill can sense when a living thing is moving at the bottom of the river. Its bubble-patterned belly serves as camouflage when it swims.

BURMY

Type: Bug
Height: 0' 08"
Weight: 7.5 lbs.

Burmy creates a cloak for itself out of whatever materials it can find. The cloak protects it from chilly temperatures and shields it in battle.

WORMADAM

Type: Bug-Grass
Height: 1' 08"
Weight: 14.3 lbs.

The cloak it wore as Burmy becomes a permanent part of Wormadam's body. Its appearance is determined by its surroundings at the time of Evolution.

MOTHIM

Type: Bug-Flying
Height: 2' 11"
Weight: 51.4 lbs.

Mothim loves the taste of Combee's honey. Sometimes it will raid a hive at night to steal the sweet substance.

SURSKIT

Type: Bug-Water
Height: 1' 08"
Weight: 3.7 lbs.

When Surskit move across the surface of the water, they look like they're on skates. Sometimes they can be seen skating on puddles after a rainstorm.

MASQUERAIN

Type: Bug-Flying
Height: 2' 07"
Weight: 7.9 lbs.

The eye patterns on Masquerain's large antennas distract attackers. Its four wings let it fly in any direction, including sideways and backward, or hover in midair.

MAGIKARP

Type: Water
Height: 2' 11"
Weight: 22.0 lbs.

Magikarp is widely regarded as the weakest Pokémon in the world. It lacks both speed and strength.

GYARADOS

Type: Water-Flying
Height: 21' 04"
Weight: 518.1 lbs.

The enormous and violent Gyarados can destroy whole villages if it becomes enraged.

CORPHISH

Type: Water
Height: 2' 00"
Weight: 25.4 lbs.

The hardy Corphish can thrive even in very polluted rivers. Once its pincers catch hold of something, it never lets go.

CRAWDAUNT

Type: Water-Dark
Height: 3' 07"
Weight: 72.3 lbs.

Feisty and territorial, Crawdaunt uses its pincers to fling any intruders out of the pond where it lives.

GOLDEEN

Type: Water
Height: 2' 00"
Weight: 33.1 lbs.

Because of the elegant waving of its graceful fins, Goldeen is known as the water dancer. It uses its horn for protection.

SEAKING

Type: Water
Height: 4' 03"
Weight: 86.0 lbs.

Using its powerful horn, Seaking can carve out holes in river rocks to make a nest. It swims upstream during the autumn.

CARVANHA

Type: Water-Dark
Height: 2' 07"
Weight: 45.9 lbs.

Carvanha swarm around any boat that enters its territory, ripping at their hulls in a furious attack. The rivers where they live are surrounded by dense jungle.

SHARPEDO

Type: Water-Dark
Height: 5' 11"
Weight: 195.8 lbs.

Sharpedo can pierce thick sheet metal with its teeth. Its streamlined body can cut through the water at seventy-five MPH.

LITLEO

Type: Fire-Normal
Height: 2' 00"
Weight: 29.8 lbs.

When Litleo is ready to get stronger, it leaves its pride to live alone. During a battle, its mane radiates intense heat.

PYROAR

Type: Fire-Normal
Height: 4' 11"
Weight: 179.7 lbs.

Pyroar live together in prides, led by the male whose fiery mane is the biggest. The females of the pride guard the young.

PSYDUCK

Type: Water
Height: 2' 07"
Weight: 43.2 lbs.

Psyduck is always suffering from a headache. The intensity of the headache amplifies its mystical powers.

GOLDUCK

Type: Water
Height: 5' 07"
Weight: 168.9 lbs.

Because of its webbed forelegs, Golduck is an excellent swimmer. When its forehead begins to glow, it can use its mystical powers.

FARFETCH'D

Type: Normal-Flying
Height: 2' 07"
Weight: 33.1 lbs.

Farfetch'd always carries its trusty plant stalk. It can brandish the stalk like a weapon or use it to build a nest.

RIOLU

Type: Fighting
Height: 2' 04"
Weight: 44.5 lbs.

The aura surrounding Riolu's body indicates its emotional state. It alters the shape of this aura to communicate.

LUCARIO

Type: Fighting-Steel
Height: 3' 11"
Weight: 119.0 lbs.

Sensing the auras that all beings emanate allows Lucario to read their minds and predict their movements. It is also very sensitive to others' emotions.

RALTS

Type: Psychic-Fairy
Height: 1' 04"
Weight: 14.6 lbs.

Ralts uses its pink horns to sense the emotions of those around it. Hostility sends it into hiding.

KIRLIA

Type: Psychic-Fairy
Height: 2' 07"
Weight: 44.5 lbs.

Positive emotions send Kirlia into a joyful spinning dance. It channels its Trainer's happiness into psychic power.

GARDEVOIR

Type: Psychic-Fairy
Height: 5' 03"
Weight: 106.7 lbs.

Fiercely protective of its Trainer, Gardevoir wields its strongest psychic power if that Trainer is in danger. It can also see into the future.

GALLADE

Type: Psychic-Fighting
Height: 5' 03"
Weight: 114.6 lbs.

A master of the blade, Gallade battles using the swordlike appendages that extend from its elbows.

FLABÉBÉ

Type: Fairy
Height: 0' 04"
Weight: 0.2 lbs.

Each Flabébé has a special connection with the flower it holds. They take care of their flowers and use them as an energy source.

FLOETTE

Type: Fairy
Height: 0' 08"
Weight: 2.0 lbs.

Floette keeps watch over flower beds and will rescue a flower if it starts to droop. It dances to celebrate the spring bloom.

FLORGES

Type: Fairy
Height: 3' 07"
Weight: 22.0 lbs.

Long ago, Florges were a welcome sight on castle grounds, where they would create elaborate flower gardens.

BUDEW

Type: Grass-Poison
Height: 0' 08"
Weight: 2.6 lbs.

When the weather turns cold, Budew's bud is tightly closed. In the springtime, it opens up again and gives off its pollen.

ROSELIA

Type: Grass-Poison
Height: 1' 00"
Weight: 4.4 lbs.

When a Roselia blooms in an unusual color, it's a sign that it's been drinking from a mineral-rich spring. Its hands secrete two different kinds of poison.

ROSERADE

Type: Grass-Poison
Height: 2' 11"
Weight: 32.0 lbs.

With its beautiful blooms, enticing aroma, and graceful movements, Roserade is quite enchanting—but watch out! Its arms conceal thorny whips, and the thorns carry poison.

LEDYBA

Type: Bug-Flying
Height: 3' 03"
Weight: 23.8 lbs.

In cold weather, many Ledyba swarm to the same place, forming a big cluster to keep each other warm. These timid Pokémon also tend to stick together for protection.

LEDIAN

Type: Bug-Flying
Height: 4' 07"
Weight: 78.5 lbs.

The pattern of Ledian's spots corresponds with the stars. As it flies through the night sky, it releases a powder that glows in the starlight.

COMBEE

Type: Bug-Flying
Height: 1' 00"
Weight: 12.1 lbs.

Combee are always in search of honey, which they bring to their Vespiquen leader. They cluster together to sleep in a formation that resembles a hive.

VESPIQUEN

Type: Bug-Flying
Height: 3' 11"
Weight: 84.9 lbs.

Vespiquen controls the colony that lives in its honeycomb body by releasing pheromones. It feeds the colony with honey provided by Combee.

SKITTY

Type: Normal
Height: 2' 00"
Weight: 24.3 lbs.

Anything that moves draws Skitty's attention and starts a playful game of chase. It often chases its own tail in a dizzying circle.

DELCATTY

Type: Normal
Height: 3' 07"
Weight: 71.9 lbs.

Because of its beautiful fur, Delcatty is favored by stylish Trainers. It looks for a clean and comfortable place where it can settle in to groom itself.

BULBASAUR

Type: Grass-Poison
Height: 2' 04"
Weight: 15.2 lbs.

Once it hatches, a Bulbasaur uses the seed on its back for the nutrients it needs in order to grow.

IVYSAUR

Type: Grass-Poison
Height: 3' 03"
Weight: 28.7 lbs.

When the flower bud on Ivysaur's back prepares to bloom, it swells and emits a sweet aroma.

VENUSAUR

Type: Grass-Poison
Height: 6' 07"
Weight: 220.5 lbs.

The scent of the flower on Venusaur's back intensifies after a rainy day. Other Pokémon are drawn to this fragrance.

CHARMANDER

Type: Fire
Height: 2' 00"
Weight: 18.7 lbs.

The flame on the tip of a Charmander's tail is a key to its current state. A healthy Charmander has an intense tail flame.

CHARMELEON

Type: Fire
Height: 3' 07"
Weight: 41.9 lbs.

When night falls in the rocky mountains where Charmeleon live, the fires on their tails can be seen glowing like stars.

CHARIZARD

Type: Fire-Flying
Height: 5' 07"
Weight: 199.5 lbs.

It's said that the more hard battles a Charizard has fought, the hotter its fire will burn.

SQUIRTLE

Type: Water
Height: 1' 08"
Weight: 19.8 lbs.

Squirtle hides in its shell for protection, but it can still fight back. Whenever it sees an opening, it strikes at its foe with spouts of water.

WARTORTLE

Type: Water
Height: 3' 03"
Weight: 49.6 lbs.

Wartortle's furry tail is a popular longevity symbol—this Pokémon is said to live as long as 10,000 years.

BLASTOISE

Type: Water
Height: 5' 03"
Weight: 188.5 lbs.

The rocket cannons on Blastoise's shell shoot water jets powerful enough to punch through thick steel.

SKIDDO

Type: Grass
Height: 2' 11"
Weight: 68.3 lbs.

Calm and gentle, Skiddo have been living side by side with people for many generations. They can create energy via photosynthesis.

GOGOAT

Type: Grass
Height: 5' 07"
Weight: 200.6 lbs.

This perceptive Pokémon can read its riders' feelings by paying attention to their grip on its horns. Gogoat also use their horns in battles for leadership.

PANCHAM

Type: Fighting
Height: 2' 00"
Weight: 17.6 lbs.

Pancham tries to be intimidating, but it's just too cute. When someone pats it on the head, it drops the tough-guy act and grins.

PANGORO

Type: Fighting-Dark
Height: 6' 11"
Weight: 299.8 lbs.

The leafy sprig Pangoro holds in its mouth helps the Pokémon track its opponents' movements. Taking hits in battle doesn't seem to bother it at all.

FURFROU

Type: Normal
Height: 3' 11"
Weight: 61.7 lbs.

An experienced groomer can trim Furfrou's fluffy coat into many different styles. Being groomed in this way makes the Pokémon both fancier and faster.

DODUO

Type: Normal-Flying
Height: 4' 07"
Weight: 86.4 lbs.

The two-headed Doduo could keep pace with a car on the highway. Its brains seem to use telepathy to communicate.

DODRIO

Type: Normal-Flying
Height: 5' 11"
Weight: 187.8 lbs.

With its swift beaks, Dodrio can deliver relentless pecking attacks. Its three heads display different emotions.

PLUSLE

Type: Electric
Height: 1' 04"
Weight: 9.3 lbs.

Plusle taps into telephone poles to drain their power. The pom-poms it waves when cheering for its friends are actually made of sparks.

MINUN

Type: Electric
Height: 1' 04"
Weight: 9.3 lbs.

Minun shoots out sparks to cheer its friends on. Being exposed to its electricity helps people relax and is good for their health.

GULPIN

Type: Poison
Height: 1' 04"
Weight: 22.7 lbs.

Most of Gulpin's body is made up of its stomach, so its other organs are small. The powerful enzymes in its stomach can digest anything.

SWALOT

Type: Poison
Height: 5' 07"
Weight: 176.4 lbs.

Swalot's mouth can open wide enough to swallow its food whole. When under attack, it sweats heavily, covering its opponent in the poisonous fluid.

SCRAGGY

Type: Dark-Fighting
Height: 2' 00"
Weight: 26.0 lbs.

Scraggy can pull its loose, rubbery skin up around its neck to protect itself from attacks. With its tough skull, it delivers headbutts without warning.

SCRAFTY

Type: Dark-Fighting
Height: 3' 07"
Weight: 66.1 lbs.

A group of Scrafty is led by the one with the biggest crest. Their powerful kicks can shatter concrete.

ABRA

Type: Psychic
Height: 2' 11"
Weight: 43.0 lbs.

Even when it's asleep—which is most of the time—Abra can sense an attack coming and teleport away.

KADABRA

Type: Psychic
Height: 4' 03"
Weight: 124.6 lbs.

The alpha waves Kadabra produces when it's using its powers can cause problems for nearby machinery.

ALAKAZAM

Type: Psychic
Height: 4' 11"
Weight: 105.8 lbs.

With its dizzying intellect, Alakazam remembers everything that happens to it. A supercomputer is no match for its incredible brain.

ODDISH

Type: Grass-Poison
Height: 1' 08"
Weight: 11.9 lbs.

Oddish spends the day underground, out of the sun. After dark, it comes out to stretch its roots, go for a walk, and soak up the moonlight.

GLOOM

Type: Grass-Poison
Height: 2' 07"
Weight: 19.0 lbs.

Most people find the strong odor of Gloom's honey extremely unpleasant. But there's no accounting for taste—about one in a thousand will actually enjoy the way it smells.

VILEPLUME

Type: Grass-Poison
Height: 3' 11"
Weight: 41.0 lbs.

Vileplume's enormous petals release clouds of poisonous pollen as it walks. Bigger petals hold larger stores of this toxic pollen.

BELLOSSOM

Type: Grass
Height: 1' 04"
Weight: 12.8 lbs.

When Bellossom come together to dance after a heavy rain, some say they're performing a ritual to draw the sun back into the sky.

SENTRET

Type: Normal
Height: 2' 07"
Weight: 13.2 lbs.

Sentret keep a careful eye on their surroundings, often standing up high on their tails so they can see farther. They also use their tails to drum on the ground as a warning.

FURRET

Type: Normal
Height: 5' 11"
Weight: 71.6 lbs.

Because Furret are so long and thin, other Pokémon can't fit into their nests. In battle, they use their superior speed to outmaneuver opponents.

NINCADA

Type: Bug-Ground
Height: 1' 08"
Weight: 12.1 lbs.

Nincada live underground, so their eyes aren't well developed. They use their antennas to sense their surroundings as they feed on tree roots.

NINJASK

Type: Bug-Flying
Height: 2' 07"
Weight: 26.5 lbs.

At top speeds, Ninjask move so fast that they're hard to see. When they find a tree with delicious sap, they gather to feed.

SHEDINJA

Type: Bug-Ghost
Height: 2' 07"
Weight: 2.6 lbs.

Some believe that looking into the crack on Shedinja's back puts your spirit in danger. Under certain circumstances, it appears alongside Ninjask when Nincada evolves.

ESPURR

Type: Psychic
Height: 1' 00"
Weight: 7.7 lbs.

Espurr emits powerful psychic energy from organs in its ears. It has to fold its ears down to keep the power contained.

MEOWSTIC

Type: Psychic
Height: 2' 00"
Weight: 18.7 lbs.

When Meowstic unfolds its ears, the psychic blast created by the eyeball patterns inside can pulverize heavy machinery. It keeps its ears tightly folded unless it's in danger.

KECLEON

Type: Normal
Height: 3' 03"
Weight: 48.5 lbs.

A master of camouflage, Kecleon can alter its coloring to blend in with any surroundings. However, its zigzag pattern stays the same.

HONEDGE

Type: Steel-Ghost
Height: 2' 07"
Weight: 4.4 lbs.

Beware when approaching a Honedge! Those foolish enough to wield it like a sword will quickly find themselves wrapped in its blue cloth and drained of energy.

DOUBLADE

Type: Steel-Ghost
Height: 2' 07"
Weight: 9.9 lbs.

The two swords that make up Doublade's body fight together in intricate slashing patterns that bewilder even accomplished swordsmen.

AEGISLASH

Type: Steel-Ghost
Height: 5' 07"
Weight: 116.8 lbs.

Aegislash has long been seen as a symbol of royalty. In olden days, these Pokémon often accompanied the king.

VENIPEDE

Type: Bug-Poison
Height: 1' 04"
Weight: 11.7 lbs.

Venipede uses the feelers at both ends of its body to explore its surroundings. It's extremely aggressive, and its bite is poisonous.

WHIRLIPEDE

Type: Bug-Poison
Height: 3' 11"
Weight: 129.0 lbs.

Covered in a sturdy shell, Whirlipede doesn't move much unless it's attacked. Then it leaps into action, spinning at high velocity and smashing into the attacker.

SCOLIPEDE

Type: Bug-Poison
Height: 8' 02"
Weight: 442.0 lbs.

The claws near Scolipede's head can be used to grab, immobilize, and poison its opponent. It moves quickly when chasing down enemies.

AUDINO

Type: Normal
Height: 3' 07"
Weight: 68.3 lbs.

With the sensitive feelers on their ears, Audino can listen to people's heartbeats to pick up on their current state. Egg-hatching can be predicted as well.

SMEARGLE

Type: Normal
Height: 3' 11"
Weight: 127.9 lbs.

Smeargle use their tails like paintbrushes to draw thousands of different territorial markings. The footprints on their backs were left there by fellow Smeargle.

CROAGUNK

Type: Poison-Fighting
Height: 2' 04"
Weight: 50.7 lbs.

Croagunk produces its distinctive croaking sound by inflating the poison sacs in its cheeks. The sound often startles an opponent so it can get in a poisonous jab.

TOXICROAK

Type: Poison-Fighting
Height: 4' 03"
Weight: 97.9 lbs.

Toxicroak's dangerous poison is stored in its throat sac and delivered through the claws on its knuckles.

DUCKLETT

Type: Water-Flying
Height: 1' 08"
Weight: 12.1 lbs.

Skilled swimmers, Ducklett dive underwater in search of delicious peat moss. When enemies approach, they kick up water with their wings to cover their retreat.

SWANNA

Type: Water-Flying
Height: 4' 03"
Weight: 53.4 lbs.

In the evening, a flock of Swanna performs an elegant dance around its leader. Their exceptional stamina and wing strength allow them to fly thousands of miles at a time.

SPRITZEE

Type: Fairy
Height: 0' 08"
Weight: 1.1 lbs.

Long ago, this Pokémon was popular among the nobility for its lovely scent. Instead of spraying perfume, ladies would keep a Spritzee close at hand.

AROMATISSE

Type: Fairy
Height: 2' 07"
Weight: 34.2 lbs.

Aromatisse uses its powerful scent as a weapon in battle. It can overpower an opponent with a strategic stench.

SWIRLIX

Type: Fairy
Height: 1' 04"
Weight: 7.7 lbs.

Swirlix loves to snack on sweets. Its sugary eating habits have made its white fur sweet and sticky, just like cotton candy.

SLURPUFF

Type: Fairy
Height: 2' 07"
Weight: 11.0 lbs.

Pastry chefs love having a Slurpuff in the kitchen. With its incredibly sensitive nose, it can tell exactly when a dessert is baked to perfection.

VOLBEAT

Type: Bug
Height: 2' 04"
Weight: 39.0 lbs.

Volbeat flashes the light on its tail to send messages to others at night. The scent of Illumise makes it very happy.

ILLUMISE

Type: Bug
Height: 2' 00"
Weight: 39.0 lbs.

Illumise gives off a sweet scent that attracts Volbeat by the dozen. It uses this scent to direct their light patterns.

HOPPIP

Type: Grass-Flying
Height: 1' 04"
Weight: 1.1 lbs.

Hoppip's body is light enough to float on the wind. If it wants to stay on the ground, it has to hold on tight with its feet. Large groups of Hoppip are said to be a sign of spring.

SKIPLOOM

Type: Grass-Flying
Height: 2' 00"
Weight: 2.2 lbs.

Skiploom opens its petals wide to soak up the sun. The blossom on its head responds to temperature, closing up when it's cold.

JUMPLUFF

Type: Grass-Flying
Height: 2' 07"
Weight: 6.6 lbs.

While drifting on the breeze, Jumpluff can control its direction with its fluffy appendages. By doing this, it can travel anywhere the wind blows.

MUNCHLAX

Type: Normal
Height: 2' 00"
Weight: 231.5 lbs.

Munchlax's long fur is a perfect place to hide snacks. With this permanent food stash, it never goes hungry.

SNORLAX

Type: Normal
Height: 6' 11"
Weight: 1014.1 lbs.

Snorlax spends most of its time eating and sleeping. Its impressive powers of digestion are unfazed by mold or rot on the food it eats.

WHISMUR

Type: Normal
Height: 2' 00"
Weight: 35.9 lbs.

When threatened, Whismur drives the attacker away with a cry as loud as a jet engine. It becomes quiet when the covers on its ears are closed.

LOUDRED

Type: Normal
Height: 3' 03"
Weight: 89.3 lbs.

A shout from a Loudred produces shock waves powerful enough to topple a big truck. When it starts stomping its feet, it's getting pumped up for battle.

EXPLOUD

Type: Normal
Height: 4' 11"
Weight: 185.2 lbs.

The ports all over Exploud's body create different sounds when air blows through them. Its battle cry shakes the ground around it and can be heard miles away.

MEDITITE

Type: Fighting-Psychic
Height: 2' 00"
Weight: 24.7 lbs.

When Meditite levitates, it's using meditation to enhance its powers. Training in the mountains sharpens its focus.

MEDICHAM

Type: Fighting-Psychic
Height: 4' 03"
Weight: 69.4 lbs.

Medicham can predict what its opponent will do next. It eludes the incoming attack with graceful movements, then strikes back.

ZUBAT

Type: Poison-Flying
Height: 2' 07"
Weight: 16.5 lbs.

Zubat live in dark caves, where they find their way with echolocation, bouncing their ultrasonic cries off nearby objects to sense their surroundings. They have no eyes.

GOLBAT

Type: Poison-Flying
Height: 5' 03"
Weight: 121.3 lbs.

With its four sharp fangs, Golbat feeds on living beings. Darkness gives it an advantage in battle, and it prefers to attack on pitch-black nights.

CROBAT

Type: Poison-Flying
Height: 5' 11"
Weight: 165.3 lbs.

Hunting in darkness, Crobat can maintain absolute silence. Its four wings let it fly quickly without sound.

AXEW

Type: Dragon
Height: 2' 00"
Weight: 39.7 lbs.

If one of Axew's tusks breaks off, it quickly regrows, even stronger and sharper than before. It uses its tusks to crush berries and mark territory.

FRAXURE

Type: Dragon
Height: 3' 03"
Weight: 79.4 lbs.

Fraxure clash in intense battles over territory. After a battle is over, they always remember to sharpen their tusks on smooth stones so they'll be ready for the next battle.

HAXORUS

Type: Dragon
Height: 5' 11"
Weight: 232.6 lbs.

Haxorus can cut through steel with its mighty tusks, which stay sharp no matter what. Its body is heavily armored.

KALOS CHALLENGE

Have you got what it takes to be a Pokémon Trainer? Ash has come a long way since he started on the path to becoming a Pokémon Master. As he travels around Kalos, he is learning new skills and building up his Pokémon knowledge. Take this test to see if you can help Ash on his journey to becoming a Pokémon Master.

1. Name the three subregions of Kalos.

2. What is the first Pokémon that Ash catches in Kalos?

3. How many Gym Badges must a Trainer earn before he or she can challenge the Kalos Elite Four?

4. What type (or types) of Pokémon is Dedenne?

5
Who is the famous Pokémon researcher based in the Kalos region?
6
Where is the Lumiose City Gym located?
7
Name the three first partner Pokémon Trainers must choose from in the Kalos region.
1
2
3
8
The three Legendary Pokémon found so far in Kalos have names beginning with X, Y and Z. Who are they?
X
Y
Z
9
Which Pokémon rushes to help Pikachu in his first Kalos battle against Jessie's Wobbuffet?
10
What is Serena's mother famous for?

THE ROAD TO SANTALUNE

START!

Ash, Clemont, and Bonnie are on their way to Santalune City for Ash's first Gym battle.

Ash can't wait to get there, but first the new friends have a few Pokémon adventures to deal with, plus a battle with their favorite villains—Team Rocket! Help the traveling party get to Santalune and catch their new Pokémon friend on the way.

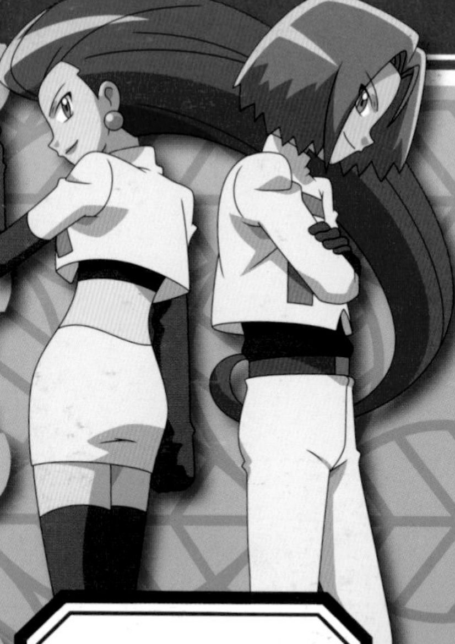

Who is the Pokémon that joins Ash and his friends? What type of Pokémon is it?

POKÉMON:

TYPE:

FINISH!

KALOS WORD SEARCH

P D J L K W H S U Z C V S Y L F O Y
R J I W O M Y F D G L O N A E K D T
I R S U H C A K I P L C V N O V Y I
S C T A I V D Q Y A E R N Q L T S C
M T H O N R I K K E I E J C U G S E
T V R H R T D C C Q K P A D N H E S
O H V F A E A V T I A G C B Y F Y O
W L V P V F T L N O O T K V Y M V I
E P P B F M U N U C R K V B T R I M
R A B K T P V T E N F Y E H C Y L U
R H Y H O R N R A C E T R A C K L L
R Y H L D T I Z V N N F C O B P A S
F Q K C G K X N Q V T O O G A V G Q
C Y L L A G E C I T Y P M R U D E I
Y T I C E N U L A T N A S É E V I E
F N L L W J V X C E Z S U E K S R Z
R J Y K T J O U E Q N D U F H O T T
S L C R H V U F H N F U J D Z C P U

Kalos is a breathtaking region of many different terrains—mountains, rivers, cliffs, marshes, forests, and beaches. The diverse geography adds exciting challenges to Ash and his friends' journey.

Find ten Kalos region locations and four special Pokémon friends above. Remember, the words can run in any direction—vertically, horizontally, diagonally, or backward. To make the challenge more difficult, try and complete the search in ten minutes!

- LUMIOSE CITY
- PRISM TOWER
- SANTALUNE CITY
- ODYSSEY VILLAGE
- POKÉMON CENTER
- CYLLAGE CITY
- KALOS
- RHYHORN RACE TRACK
- SANTALUNE FOREST
- VICTORY ROAD
- PIKACHU
- FROAKIE
- CHESPIN
- FENNEKIN

BATTLE ARENA!

In order to compete in the Pokémon League, Ash must participate in battles and earn Gym Badges in each region he travels through. Ash has already won lots of Gym Badges and is well on his way to achieving his dream. He can't wait to get into the battle arena to show off his fighting skills!

THE POKÉMON LEAGUE

The Pokémon League is the official group that organizes Gym battle competitions for registered Pokémon Trainers. It oversees all the regional leagues. In order to take part in regional competitions, Ash must win a certain number of Gym Badges to show that he's defeated that region's Gym Leaders.

THE KALOS LEAGUE

This League is made up of eight Kalos Gym Leaders, the Kalos Elite Four members, and the Kalos Champion. Ash has to earn eight Gym Badges by defeating the eight Gym Leaders to qualify to challenge the Elite Four.

ASH'S FIRST KALOS GYM BATTLE:

SANTALUNE CITY GYM

ASH'S POKÉMON

VIOLA'S POKÉMON

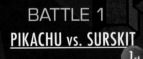

BATTLE 1
PIKACHU vs. SURSKIT
1st

BATTLE 2
FLETCHLING vs. SURSKIT
1st

BATTLE 3
FLETCHLING vs. VIVILLON
1st

CHAMPION: VIOLA'S VIVILLON

ASH'S REMATCH WITH VIOLA:

SANTALUNE CITY GYM

ASH'S POKÉMON

VIOLA'S POKÉMON

BATTLE 1
PIKACHU vs. SURSKIT
1st

BATTLE 2
FLETCHLING vs. SURSKIT
1st

BATTLE 3
PIKACHU vs. VIVILLON
1st

CHAMPION: ASH'S PIKACHU

BADGE EARNED

To challenge the Gym Leader at Lumiose City, Ash will have to earn four Gym Badges. One down, three to go! Cyllage City Gym, here Ash comes . . .

A BLUSTERY SANTALUNE GYM BATTLE

Serena always remembered the time she met and made friends with Ash a few years before at a Pokémon summer camp.

Today, she was going to travel to Santalune City. She was determined to try and meet Ash again to see if he remembered her.

Meanwhile, Ash, Clemont, and Bonnie had arrived in Santalune City and were making their way to the Gym so Ash could challenge his first Gym Leader in the Kalos region.

"Wow, we made it! Hey, guys, we're here," cried Ash. "Look out, Santalune Gym! I'm gonna get my first Kalos badge from you!"

"Now, if I remember my facts correctly, the Santalune Gym Leader specializes in Bug-type Pokémon," said Clemont, looking up at the big building in front of them.

"I can't wait to go inside, it's gonna be fun!" Bonnie giggled.

Just then a girl and a Helioptile appeared at the Gym entrance.

"Hey, Alexa! I didn't know you were here!" Ash laughed.

"I guessed you'd be here soon, and I thought I'd wait for you. Welcome!" replied Alexa.

"I didn't know that you already knew the Gym Leader, Ash," said Clemont.

"I don't," replied Ash. "This is Alexa, my Pokémon journalist friend. Alexa, meet my new friends, Clemont and Bonnie."

Alexa showed the group into the Gym. "My younger sister, Viola, is the Gym Leader . . . ah, here she is. She's also a fabulous photographer!"

Ash and his friends stared at all the wonderful photographs hanging in the entrance hall.

"These are great!" sighed Clemont.

"Ah, thank you, so much," replied Viola. "These are just a few of my pictures . . . Anyway, Ash, Alexa tells me you want to challenge me to a Gym Battle."

"I do!" cried Ash. "How about it?"

"Cool. Let's go!" replied Viola.

Everyone followed Viola out into the battle arena courtyard. Alexa, Clemont, and Bonnie stood on the sidelines, ready to watch the battle. There was a spark of tension in the air as Viola and Ash prepared themselves and the referee called out the rules.

"The Gym Battle between Ash, the challenger, and Viola, the Santalune Gym Leader, will now begin! Each side will have the use of two Pokémon, and the battle will be over when either Trainer's Pokémon are unable to continue! Only the challenger may substitute Pokémon."

Viola unleashed her Pokémon, Surskit, the Pond Skater Pokémon. "My lens is always focused on victory!" she yelled. "I won't let anything ruin this shot! Go, Surskit!"

Ash checked his Pokédex.

"Surskit can walk on water as if it were skating. It attacks prey with the sweet aroma it produces."

"I'm gonna start off with Pikachu!" Ash yelled back.

"Let the battle . . . begin!" shouted the referee.

In a flash, Pikachu launched the battle with a Quick Attack Move. Viola instructed Surskit to use Protect as the Pokémon dashed around the arena, sliding and slicing through the air. The battle was heating up!

When Pikachu's Iron Tail didn't work, Ash instructed his Pokémon to use Electro Ball. But when Viola got Surskit to use Ice Beam, the feisty Pikachu's electricity was no match.

Pikachu was flung to the ground as Surskit's Ice Beam turned the battle arena into an ice rink.

"Hang in there, Pikachu!" yelled Ash.

"You can do it!" cried Clemont and Bonnie from the sidelines.

Poor Pikachu was exhausted. Ash knew he had to do something pretty quick, so he told Pikachu to use his signature Thunderbolt move. But as the bolt of electricity sparked across the arena toward Surskit, Pikachu flew through the air and slammed onto the ice. Ash gasped as Surskit's Signal Beam blasted Pikachu.

Pikachu lay on the ground, battered and bruised.

"Pikachu is unable to battle. Surskit wins!" called the referee.

Ash ran to Pikachu's side. "You were great out there. Thanks, buddy!" he whispered as he carefully moved Pikachu to safety. Ash turned back to Viola.

"You trained Pikachu well, but it still has quite a long way to go before it can beat my Surskit," Viola said.

Ash was not one to give up. "I'll beat it now!" he shouted. "With this Pokémon—Fletchling, let's go!"

Clemont started to tell Bonnie and Alexa that a Flying-type Pokémon like Fletchling should have an advantage over Surskit when he was interrupted by Serena's arrival.

"Can I watch them battle?" she asked.

"Of course!" replied Alexa. "Welcome."

"It's getting really good!" Bonnie giggled as the second battle got under way.

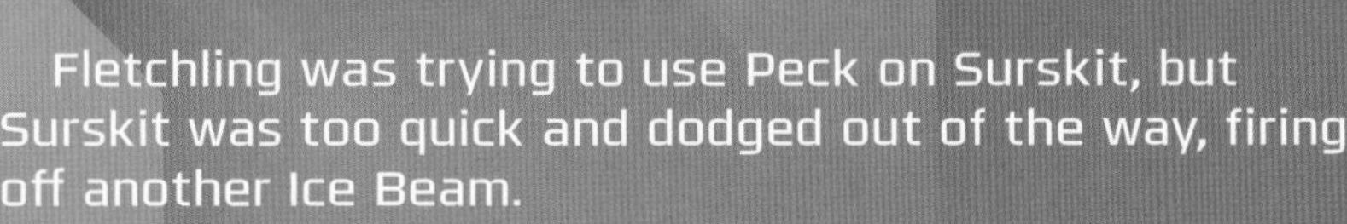

Fletchling was trying to use Peck on Surskit, but Surskit was too quick and dodged out of the way, firing off another Ice Beam.

In a whirl of wings and legs, Fletchling and Surskit battled hard, throwing out different moves.

Surskit managed to dodge Fletchling's Double Team attack, shooting out a Sticky Web that narrowly missed trapping Fletchling.

The audience was captivated. Which Pokémon was going to win this battle? They seemed so evenly matched. Then, in a surprise move, Fletchling used Razor Wind and knocked Surskit out.

"Surskit is unable to battle. Fletchling wins!" shouted out the referee.

Clemont, Bonnie, and Serena jumped up and down in excitement.

"Cool!" cried Bonnie. "Did you see how awesome Ash battles?!" Serena smiled.

"Now both sides have one Pokémon left. Ash just might win this!" said Clemont, grinning happily.

Ash and Viola were ready to battle again.

"Time to beat your Pokémon and get my hands on a Kalos badge!" said Ash.

"It's not going to be that easy. My Gym Leader pride's on the line! Let's do this . . . Vivillon!" Viola replied as she unleashed her second Pokémon. It flew up into the air, flapping its brilliantly multicolored wings.

"Woah! A Scale Pokémon!" cried Ash, checking his Pokédex. "Vivillon are skillfully able to find a source of water. Okay, Fletchling. Peck!"

A new battle raged in the air above the frozen battle arena.

Vivillon dodged Fletchling's Peck and launched Psychic. Poor Fletchling didn't know what had hit it.

Just as Fletchling was about to retaliate, Vivillon used Gust. Fletchling didn't have time to recover before it was blown straight into the Sticky Web left by Surskit.

"Break free, Fletchling!" Ash cried. "You can do it!"

Fletchling valiantly struggled to get out of the Sticky Web, but suddenly there was a massive burst of light and a surge of heat, and Fletchling was blasted to the ground.

The audience groaned as the referee announced the end of the battle.

"Fletchling is unable to battle. Vivillon wins, which means the victor is Viola, the Gym Leader!"

Ash clutched Fletchling to his chest. He was very upset. "I know I lost. But . . . I'll come back here stronger! When I do, I hope you'll let me have a rematch."

Viola smiled. "I'll be looking forward to it. Come back anytime!"

Clemont grabbed Ash's arm. "We need to get Fletchling and Pikachu to a Pokémon Center, quickly. They're in pretty bad shape."

Ash, Bonnie, and Clemont rushed off carrying the injured Pokémon. A disappointed Serena looked on. As she was wondering how and when she was going to introduce herself to Ash, she spied his backpack laying on the ground by the

side of the arena. She picked it up and set off after him.

At the Pokémon Center, Ash, Clemont, and Bonnie were waiting to find out how Pikachu and Fletchling were doing when Serena burst through the entrance doors.

"Oh, hi, sorry to interrupt, but I think this is yours," Serena said, handing the backpack over to Ash.

Ash looked surprised. He smiled at Serena. "Er, thanks," he mumbled. "Hi, I'm Ash and these are my friends."

"Yeah, I know. I'm Serena. Do you remember . . . ?" Serena started to say.

Just then, Nurse Joy hurried in, holding Ash's two Pokémon. "They're both fully recovered and feeling fine," she said.

"Thank you so much, Nurse Joy," said Ash, beaming with happiness.

"Oh, Nurse Joy," interrupted Serena. "Could you take a look at my Pokémon, too?" She put Fennekin on the counter.

"I'd be glad to," said Nurse Joy. "Wait here while I perform a thorough exam."

"Whoa! What's that? Never seen that Pokémon before," said Ash.

"It's a Fox Pokémon. I got it from Professor Sycamore," replied Serena. "I'm a new Trainer and I've just started my journey."

"Great! Come and watch us training, if you like," said Ash. "We've got to find a way to deal with Vivillon's Gust and Surskit's Ice Beam and Sticky Web if we're going to stand a chance in the rematch against Viola!"

Will Ash be able to come up with a strategy to defeat Viola and win his first Kalos region Gym badge?

FIND OUT ON PAGE 48!

KALOS ADVENTURE CROSSWORD

All great Pokémon Trainers are super-alert and quick-thinking, with sharp powers of observation. Are you ready to be a Pokémon Trainer? Test your knowledge of Ash's adventures in Kalos by filling in this tricky crossword. Use the clues below to help you.

1 2 3 4 5 6 7 8 9 10

DOWN

1. Name of Clemont's robot
3. Final Evolution of Froakie
4. Professor who has a research lab in Lumiose City
6. Number of Gym Badges Ash needs to earn to compete at the Lumiose City Gym
9. Team Rocket's talking Pokémon

ACROSS

2. Wild Pokémon that tries to attack Serena in the Santalune Forest
5. Spikes Pokémon that can be raced in Odyssey Village
7. Pokémon dealer who specializes in Scatterbug, Spewpa, and Vivillon
8. Kalos' celebrated Pokémon groomer
10. Gym Leader Viola's journalist sister

Gotta Catch 'Em All!

It's never easy trying to catch a Pokémon, even with the help of your friends. These clever little creatures can be very tricky at times!

Look at the picture grid below. Ash has managed to catch six different Kalos Pokémon, and six of each type. Unfortunately, sneaky Rocket Team has managed to steal twelve Pokémon. Help Ash get them all back to complete his sets. Remember, each of the six Pokémon must only appear once on each horizontal and vertical line. Draw each missing Pokémon into the correct square on the grid.

WHO'S WHO?

Do you know your Xerneas from your Yveltal? Your Inkay from your Helioptile? Well, now here's your chance to show what a super-skilled and observant Pokémon Trainer you are!
Look at the pictures below. Which Pokémon species can you spy?

1

This Shellfish Pokémon has cannons on its shell.

ANSWER:

2

A cute Fairy-type Pokémo who sings soothing lullab

ANSWER:

3

This Fairy-type Pokémon can float using its special buoyant tail.

ANSWER:

4

This fiery Pokémon has a flame at the tip of its tail.

ANSWER:

5

A playful Fighting-type Pokémon that's just too cute to be intimidating.

ANSWER:

6

Despite its spiky appearan this Pokémon has a gentle nature and doesn't like confrontation.

ANSWER:

7

This fluffy Pokémon loves being groomed.

ANSWER:

8

This Bug-type Pokémon ca paralyze its attacker with cloud of black powder.

ANSWER:

Pikachu & First Partner Pokémon

POKÉMON™

POKÉMON™

Meet the TRAINERS

Eevee and its EVOLUTIONS

Mega-Evolved Pokémon

POKéMON™

POKéMON™
Mega-Evolved Pokémon

Legendary and Mythical Pokémon

POKÉMON TYPE TEST

How skilled are you at spotting all the different types of Pokémon? There are eighteen types in all, and every species you come across will belong to one or even two of these types. Ash passed the test with flying colors! So, no pressure, but can you figure them all out, too? Match each Pokémon to its correct type.

Zoroark

Pumpkaboo

Squirtle

Litleo

Wigglytuff

Gogoat

Croagunk

Raichu

Glaceon

Wobbuffet

NORMAL FAIRY

WATER

GHOST GRASS

POISON FIGHTING

ELECTRIC

ICE

DARK

GRASS

PSYCHIC

FIRE NORMAL

DRIFLOON

Type: Ghost-Flying
Height: 1' 04"
Weight: 2.6 lbs.

Known as the "Signpost for Wandering Spirits," Drifloon itself was formed by spirits. It prefers humid weather and is happiest when it's floating through damp air.

DRIFBLIM

Type: Ghost-Flying
Height: 3' 11"
Weight: 33.1 lbs.

During the day, Drifblim tend to be sleepy. They take flight at dusk, but since they can't control their direction, they'll drift away wherever the wind blows them.

MIENFOO

Type: Fighting
Height: 2' 11"
Weight: 44.1 lbs.

In battle, Mienfoo never stops moving, flowing through one attack after another with grace and speed. Its claws are very sharp.

MIENSHAO

Type: Fighting
Height: 4' 07"
Weight: 78.3 lbs.

With the long, whiplike fur on its arms, Mienshao can unleash a flurry of attacks so fast they're almost invisible. Its battle combos are unstoppable.

ZANGOOSE

Type: Normal
Height: 4' 03"
Weight: 88.8 lbs.

When Zangoose smells an enemy, its fur bristles up and it wields its sharp claws. These Pokémon constantly feud with Seviper.

SEVIPER

Type: Poison
Height: 8'10"
Weight: 115.7 lbs.

Seviper keeps the blade on its poisonous tail polished to a razor-sharp edge. These Pokémon constantly feud with Zangoose.

SPOINK

Type: Psychic
Height: 2' 04"
Weight: 67.5 lbs.

The constant bouncing motion of Spoink's springy tail regulates its heartbeat. The pearl on its forehead was produced by a Clamperl.

GRUMPIG

Type: Psychic
Height: 2' 11"
Weight: 157.6 lbs.

When Grumpig does an odd little dance, it's trying to use mind control on its opponents. The black pearls on its body boost its mystical powers.

ABSOL

Type: Dark
Height: 3' 11"
Weight: 103.6 lbs.

Where Absol appears, disaster often follows. Rather than heed its warning, people sometimes blame it for whatever happens next.

INKAY

Type: Dark-Psychic
Height: 1' 04"
Weight: 7.7 lbs.

The spots on Inkay's body emit a flashing light. This light confuses its opponents, giving it a chance to escape.

MALAMAR

Type: Dark-Psychic
Height: 4'11"
Weight: 103.6 lbs.

With hypnotic compulsion, Malamar can control the actions of others, forcing them to do its will. The movement of its tentacles can put anyone watching into a trance.

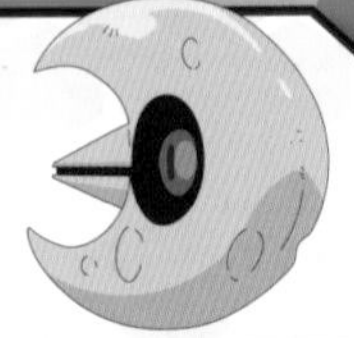

LUNATONE

Type: Rock-Psychic
Height: 3' 03"
Weight: 370.4 lbs.

Lunatone can make its opponents sleep merely by staring at them. It's most active when the moon is full.

SOLROCK

Type: Rock-Psychic
Height: 3' 11"
Weight: 339.5 lbs.

Solrock soaks up the sun's rays during the day to keep itself powered up. Its body gives off a sunny glow when it spins.

BAGON

Type: Dragon
Height: 2' 00"
Weight: 92.8 lbs.

Looking forward to the day it will be able to fly, Bagon practices by jumping from high places.

SHELGON

Type: Dragon
Height: 3' 07"
Weight: 243.6 lbs.

The heavy, armored shell that encases Shelgon's body protects it from attacks, but also makes it move slowly.

SALAMENCE

Type: Dragon-Flying
Height: 4' 11"
Weight: 226.2 lbs.

Salamence poses a serious threat to everything around it if it becomes enraged. Its fits of fiery destruction cannot be controlled.

WINGULL

Type: Water-Flying
Height: 2' 00"
Weight: 20.9 lbs.

Wingull build nests on the sides of steep cliffs by the sea. Stretching out their long wings, they soar on the ocean breeze.

PELIPPER

Type: Water-Flying
Height: 3' 11"
Weight: 61.7 lbs.

With its enormous bill, Pelipper can scoop up large quantities of water and food from the sea. It's also been known to rescue small Pokémon from danger by carrying them in its bill.

TAILLOW

Type: Normal-Flying
Height: 1' 00"
Weight: 5.1 lbs.

Taillow don't like the cold and will fly nearly 200 miles in a single day to seek out a warmer home. They show real fighting spirit in battle, even against tough opponents.

SWELLOW

Type: Normal-Flying
Height: 2' 04"
Weight: 43.7 lbs.

Soaring gracefully through the sky, Swellow will go into a steep dive if it spots food on the ground. Its prominent tail feathers stand straight up when it's in good health.

BINACLE

Type: Rock-Water
Height: 1' 08"
Weight: 68.3 lbs.

Binacle live in pairs, two on the same rock. They comb the beach for seaweed to eat.

BARBARACLE

Type: Rock-Water
Height: 4' 03"
Weight: 211.6 lbs.

When seven Binacle come together to fight as one, a Barbaracle is formed. The head gives the orders, but the limbs don't always listen.

DWEBBLE

Type: Bug-Rock
Height: 1' 00"
Weight: 32.0 lbs.

Using a special liquid from its mouth, Dwebble hollows out a rock to use as its shell. It becomes very anxious without a proper rock.

CRUSTLE

Type: Bug-Rock
Height: 4' 07"
Weight: 440.9 lbs.

Because Crustle carries a heavy slab of rock everywhere it goes, its legs are extremely strong. Battles between them are determined by whose rock breaks first.

TENTACOOL

Type: Water-Poison
Height: 2' 11"
Weight: 100.3 lbs.

Water makes up most of Tentacool's body. It drifts with the current in areas where the sea is shallow.

TENTACRUEL

Type: Water-Poison
Height: 5' 03"
Weight: 121.3 lbs.

Eighty tentacles, equipped with painful venom, extend from Tentacruel's body. It can pull them in to make itself smaller or lengthen them to attack.

WAILMER

Type: Water
Height: 6' 07"
Weight: 286.6 lbs.

Wailmer swallows seawater to make its round body even rounder and its playful bounces even higher. It releases the seawater in a forceful spray from its blowholes.

WAILORD

Type: Water
Height: 47' 07"
Weight: 877.4 lbs.

When Wailord leaps from the water in a mighty breach and then crashes down again, the shock wave it creates is sometimes enough to knock an opponent out.

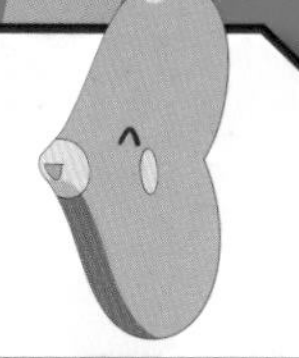

LUVDISC

Type: Water
Height: 2' 00"
Weight: 19.2 lbs.

During certain times of the year, so many Luvdisc gather around a single reef that the water appears to turn pink. They are rumored to bring endless love to couples who find them.

SKRELP

Type: Poison-Water
Height: 1' 08"
Weight: 16.1 lbs.

Skrelp disguises itself as rotten kelp to hide from enemies. It defends itself by spraying a poisonous liquid.

DRAGALGE

Type: Poison-Dragon
Height: 5' 11"
Weight: 179.7 lbs.

Toxic and territorial, Dragalge defend their homes from anything that enters. Even large ships aren't safe from their poison.

CLAUNCHER

Type: Water
Height: 1' 08"
Weight: 18.3 lbs.

Clauncher shoots water from its claws with a force that can pulverize rock. Its range is great enough to knock flying Pokémon out of the air.

CLAWITZER

Type: Water
Height: 4' 03"
Weight: 77.8 lbs.

Clawitzer's giant claw can expel massive jets of water at high speed. It fires the water forward to attack, or backward to propel itself through the sea.

STARYU

Type: Water
Height: 2' 07"
Weight: 76.1 lbs.

The red core at the middle of Staryu's body can be seen flashing at night. As long as this core is whole, it can regenerate from any damage.

STARMIE

Type: Water-Psychic
Height: 3' 07"
Weight: 176.4 lbs.

The gemlike core at Starmie's center emits light of many colours. It is also thought to produce radio waves at night.

SHELLDER

Type: Water
Height: 1' 00"
Weight: 8.8 lbs.

When Shellder's shell is open, its soft body is vulnerable to attacks. After opening, it can clamp down fiercely on an opponent, but the risk is often too great.

CLOYSTER

Type: Water-Ice
Height: 4' 11"
Weight: 292.1 lbs.

Cloyster with sharp spikes on their shells tend to live in a part of the sea where the current is particularly strong. They keep their shells closed except to attack.

QWILFISH

Type: Water-Poison
Height: 1' 08"
Weight: 8.6 lbs.

Qwilfish's body bristles all over with venomous spikes. When it puffs itself up by rapidly sucking in large quantities of water, the spikes shoot outward.

HORSEA

Type: Water
Height: 1' 04"
Weight: 17.6 lbs.

When threatened, Horsea covers its retreat by spitting a murky cloud of ink. It prefers to nest in coral.

SEADRA

Type: Water
Height: 3' 11"
Weight: 55.1 lbs.

The bristling spikes that cover Seadra's body are very sharp, so touching it is not recommended. It can swim in reverse by flapping its large fins.

KINGDRA

Type: Water-Dragon
Height: 5' 11"
Weight: 335.1 lbs.

Kingdra lives quite comfortably in the crushing depths of the ocean. When it yawns, it sucks in so much water that a whirlpool forms on the surface.

RELICANTH

Type: Water-Rock
Height: 3' 03"
Weight: 51.6 lbs.

The ancient Pokémon Relicanth has existed for 100 million years without changing. Deep-sea explorers discovered it at the bottom of the ocean.

SANDILE

Type: Ground-Dark
Height: 2' 04"
Weight: 33.5 lbs.

Sandile travels just below the surface of the desert sand, with only its nose and eyes sticking out. The warmth of the sand keeps it from getting too cold.

KROKOROK

Type: Ground-Dark
Height: 3' 03"
Weight: 73.6 lbs.

The membranes that cover Krokorok's eyes not only protect the eyes during sandstorms, but also act like heat sensors, enabling it to navigate in total darkness.

KROOKODILE

Type: Ground-Dark
Height: 4' 11"
Weight: 212.3 lbs.

Krookodile's formidable jaws are capable of crunching up cars. Triggered into violence by nearby movement, Krookodile will clamp on inescapably with all the might of those jaws.

HELIOPTILE

Type: Electric-Normal
Height: 1' 08"
Weight: 13.2 lbs.

The frills on Helioptile's head soak up sunlight and create electricity. In this way, they can generate enough energy to keep them going without food.

HELIOLISK

Type: Electric-Normal
Height: 3' 03"
Weight: 46.3 lbs.

Heliolisk generates electricity by spreading its frill out wide to soak up the sun. It uses this energy to boost its speed.

HIPPOPOTAS

Type: Ground
Height: 2' 07"
Weight: 109.1 lbs.

Hippopotas lives in a dry environment. Its body gives off sand instead of sweat, and this sandy shield keeps it protected from water and germs.

HIPPOWDON

Type: Ground
Height: 6' 07"
Weight: 661.4 lbs.

Hippowdon stores sand inside its body and expels it through the ports on its sides to create a twisting sandstorm in battle.

RHYHORN

Type: Ground-Rock
Height: 3' 03"
Weight: 253.5 lbs.

When Rhyhorn charges, look out! It's strong enough to knock down a building, and because of its short legs, it has trouble changing direction.

RHYDON

Type: Ground-Rock
Height: 6' 03"
Weight: 264.6 lbs.

After evolving, Rhydon begins to walk upright. Its horn is strong enough to drill through boulders, and its hide is thick enough to protect it from molten lava.

RHYPERIOR

Type: Ground-Rock
Height: 7' 10"
Weight: 623.5 lbs.

Rhyperior uses the holes in its hands to bombard its opponents with rocks. Sometimes it even hurls a Geodude! Rhyperior's rocky hide is thick enough to protect it from molten lava.

ONIX

Type: Rock-Ground
Height: 28' 10"
Weight: 463.0 lbs.

When Onix is searching for food underground, it can bore through the soil at impressive speeds. Diglett sometimes live in the burrows it leaves behind.

STEELIX

Type: Steel-Ground
Height: 30' 02"
Weight: 881.8 lbs.

Steelix lives deep underground, where intense heat and pressure have compressed its body to a steely toughness. It can crunch up large rocks in its jaws.

WOOBAT

Type: Psychic-Flying
Height: 1' 04"
Weight: 4.6 lbs.

When Woobat attaches itself to something, it leaves a heart-shaped mark with its nose. The nose is also the source of its echolocation signals.

SWOOBAT

Type: Psychic-Flying
Height: 2' 11"
Weight: 23.1 lbs.

When a male Swoobat is trying to impress a female, it gives off ultrasonic waves that put everyone in a good mood. Under other circumstances, Swoobat's waves can pulverize concrete.

MACHOP

Type: Fighting
Height: 2' 07"
Weight: 43.0 lbs.

Machop lifts a Graveler like a weight to make its muscles stronger. It can throw opponents much bigger than itself.

MACHOKE

Type: Fighting
Height: 4' 11"
Weight: 155.4 lbs.

Machoke is strong enough to pick up a dump truck with one arm. It channels this strength in a helpful way, often assisting people with heavy things.

MACHAMP

Type: Fighting
Height: 5' 03"
Weight: 286.6 lbs.

With its four muscular arms, Machamp can unleash hundreds of punches a second or pin its opponent to the ground.

CUBONE

Type: Ground
Height: 1' 04"
Weight: 14.3 lbs.

Cubone wears its mother's skull as a helmet and always keeps its face hidden. When it's lonely, its cries become very loud.

MAROWAK

Type: Ground
Height: 3' 03"
Weight: 99.2 lbs.

Using bones as weapons has given Marowak a fierce temperament. It can knock out an opponent with a skillfully thrown bone.

KANGASKHAN

Type: Normal
Height: 7' 03"
Weight: 176.4 lbs.

The little one leaves the belly pouch only when it's safe to play outside. While it's out, Kangaskhan keeps careful watch.

MAWILE

Type: Steel-Fariy
Height: 2' 00"
Weight: 25.4 lbs.

The massive jaws on the back of Mawile's head are strong enough to crunch up iron beams.

TYRUNT

Type: Rock-Dragon
Height: 2' 07"
Weight: 57.3 lbs.

Tyrunt often responds to frustration by pitching a fit. This ancient Pokémon lived millions of years ago.

TYRANTRUM

Type: Rock-Dragon
Height: 8' 02"
Weight: 595.2 lbs.

Tyrantrum's enormous and powerful jaws made it the boss of its ancient world. Nothing could challenge its rule.

AMAURA

Type: Rock-Ice
Height: 4' 03"
Weight: 55.6 lbs.

In the ancient world, Amaura's cold habitat kept predators at bay. It was restored from a frozen fragment.

AURORUS

Type: Rock-Ice
Height: 8' 10"
Weight: 496.0 lbs.

With the icy crystals that line its sides, Aurorus can freeze the surrounding air and trap its foes in ice.

AERODACTYL

Type: Rock-Flying
Height: 6' 11"
Weight: 130.1 lbs.

This Pokémon was restored from an ancient piece of amber. As Aerodactyl flies, it screeches in a high-pitched voice.

FERROSEED

Type: Grass-Steel
Height: 2' 00"
Weight: 41.4 lbs.

Ferroseed use their spikes to cling to cave ceilings and absorb iron. They can also shoot those spikes to cover their escape when enemies approach.

FERROTHORN

Type: Grass-Steel
Height: 3' 03"
Weight: 242.5 lbs.

Ferrothorn swings its spiked feelers to attack. It likes to hang from the ceiling of a cave and shower spikes on anyone passing below.

SNUBBULL

Type: Fairy
Height: 2' 00"
Weight: 17.2 lbs.

Snubbull's scary face hides an affectionate and playful side. Many people think it's cute despite its fierce expression.

GRANBULL

Type: Fairy
Height: 4' 07"
Weight: 107.4 lbs.

With its giant fangs and gaping mouth, Granbull looks scary, but it's actually very timid. Its best bet in battle is to frighten an opponent into running away.

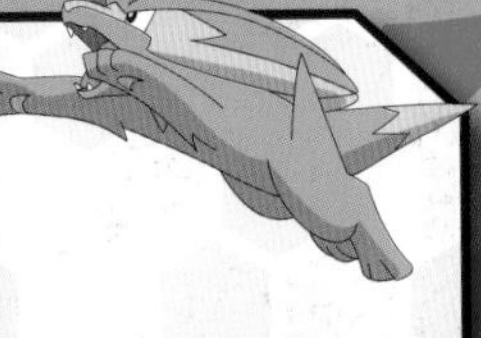

ELECTRIKE

Type: Electric
Height: 2' 00"
Weight: 33.5 lbs.

Electrike's fur soaks up static electricity. When a thunderstorm is coming, the electricity in the air makes it throw sparks.

MANECTRIC

Type: Electric
Height: 4' 11"
Weight: 88.6 lbs.

In places where lightning strikes the ground, Manectric makes its nest. Its mane gives off an electric charge.

HOUNDOUR

Type: Dark-Fire
Height: 2' 00"
Weight: 23.8 lbs.

If you hear a spine-chilling howl just at sunrise, you might have wandered into Houndour's territory.

HOUNDOOM

Type: Dark-Fire
Height: 4' 07"
Weight: 77.2 lbs.

Houndoom's eerie howl was once thought to be a bad omen. Its fiery breath causes a painful burn that never heals.

EEVEE

Type: Normal
Height: 1' 00"
Weight: 14.3 lbs.

The amazingly adaptive Eevee can evolve into many different Pokémon depending on its environment. This allows it to withstand harsh conditions.

VAPOREON

Type: Water
Height: 3' 03"
Weight: 63.9 lbs.

Vaporeon's cellular structure resembles water molecules, so it can melt away and vanish in its aquatic environment. It loves beautiful beaches.

JOLTEON

Type: Electric
Height: 2' 07"
Weight: 54.0 lbs.

When Jolteon's fur sticks straight out, it's building up an electric charge. It can gather electricity from the air around it to power its high-voltage attacks.

FLAREON

Type: Fire
Height: 2' 11"
Weight: 55.1 lbs.

The flame sac inside Flareon's body powers its intense fiery breath. When it's preparing for battle, its body temperature can reach more than 1,500 degrees Fahrenheit.

ESPEON

Type: Psychic
Height: 2' 11"
Weight: 58.4 lbs.

The incredibly sensitive fur covering Espeon's body can detect even the tiniest movement of the air. This allows it to sense changes in the weather and predict what its opponent will do next.

UMBREON

Type: Dark
Height: 3' 03"
Weight: 59.5 lbs.

Umbreon's genetic structure is influenced by moonlight. When the moon shines upon it, the rings in its fur give off a faint glow.

LEAFEON

Type: Grass
Height: 3' 03"
Weight: 56.2 lbs.

When Leafeon soaks up the sun for use in photosynthesis, it gives off clean, fresh air. It often takes naps in a sunny area to gather energy.

GLACEON

Type: Ice
Height: 2' 07"
Weight: 57.1 lbs.

The icy Glaceon has amazing control over its body temperature. It can freeze its own fur and then fire the frozen hairs like needles at an opponent.

SYLVEON

Type: Fairy
Height: 3' 03"
Weight: 51.8 lbs.

To keep others from fighting, Sylveon projects a calming aura from its feelers, which look like flowing ribbons. It wraps those ribbons around its Trainer's arm when they walk together.

EMOLGA

Type: Electric-Flying
Height: 1' 04"
Weight: 11.0 lbs.

When Emolga stretches out its limbs, the membrane connecting them spreads like a cape and allows it to glide through the air. It makes its abode high in the trees.

YANMA

Type: Bug-Flying
Height: 3' 11"
Weight: 83.8 lbs.

With its compound eyes, Yanma can see in every direction without moving its head. It can send out a shock wave from its rapidly buzzing wings.

YANMEGA

Type: Bug-Flying
Height: 6' 03"
Weight: 113.5 lbs.

With four wings on its back and two more on its tail to keep it balanced, Yanmega is capable of extremely high-speed flight. It can carry a full-grown person through the air.

HAWLUCHA

Type: Fighting-Flying
Height: 2' 07"
Weight: 47.4 lbs.

Hawlucha prefers to fight by diving at its foes from above. This aerial advantage makes up for its small size.

SIGILYPH

Type: Psychic-Flying
Height: 4' 07"
Weight: 30.9 lbs.

Sigilyph were appointed to keep watch over an ancient city. Their patrol route never varies.

GOLETT

Type: Ground-Ghost
Height: 3' 03"
Weight: 202.8 lbs.

Sculpted from clay and animated by a mysterious internal energy, Golett are the product of ancient science.

GOLURK

Type: Ground-Ghost
Height: 9' 02"
Weight: 727.5 lbs.

The seal on Golurk's chest keeps its energy contained and stops it from going wild. Long ago, these Pokémon were created as protectors.

NOSEPASS

Type: Rock
Height: 3' 03"
Weight: 213.8 lbs.

Because its nose is magnetic, Nosepass always faces north, so travelers check it like a compass. Its nose sometimes attracts metal objects that it can use as a shield.

PROBOPASS

Type: Rock-Steel
Height: 4' 07"
Weight: 749.6 lbs.

Probopass uses the strong magnetic field it generates to control the three smaller Mini-Noses attached to the sides of its body.

MAKUHITA

Type: Fighting
Height: 3' 03"
Weight: 190.5 lbs.

By repeatedly slamming its body into sturdy tree trunks, Makuhita toughens itself up for battle. Its severe training gives it a fierce fighting spirit.

HARIYAMA

Type: Fighting
Height: 7' 07"
Weight: 559.5 lbs.

Hariyama's arms are so strong that a single punch can send a heavy truck flying through the air. It challenges bigger Pokémon to tests of strength.

THROH

Type: Fighting
Height: 4' 03"
Weight: 122.4 lbs.

Throh make belts for themselves out of vines and pull those belts tight to power up their muscles. They can't resist the challenge of throwing a bigger opponent.

SAWK

Type: Fighting
Height: 4' 07"
Weight: 112.4 lbs.

Sawk go deep into the mountains to train their fighting skills relentlessly. If they are disturbed during this training, they become very angry.

STARLY

Type: Normal-Flying
Height: 1' 00"
Weight: 4.4 lbs.

Huge flocks of Starly gather in fields and mountains. In such large numbers, their wings flap with impressive power . . . and their noisy singing is quite a nuisance!

STARAVIA

Type: Normal-Flying
Height: 2' 00"
Weight: 34.2 lbs.

Staravia travel in large flocks that can be very territorial. Battles sometimes break out between two competing flocks.

STARAPTOR

Type: Normal-Flying
Height: 3' 11"
Weight: 54.9 lbs.

After evolving, Staraptor go off on their own, leaving their flocks behind. With their strong wings, they can fly with ease even when carrying a burden.

STUNKY

Type: Poison-Dark
Height: 1' 04"
Weight: 42.3 lbs.

The terrible-smelling fluid that Stunky sprays from its rear can keep others far away from it for a whole day.

SKUNTANK

Type: Poison-Dark
Height: 3' 03"
Weight: 83.8 lbs.

From the end of its tail, Skuntank can shoot a noxious fluid more than 160 feet. This fluid smells awful, and the stench only gets worse if it's not cleaned up immediately.

NIDORAN ♀

Type: Poison
Height: 1' 04"
Weight: 15.4 lbs.

Nidoran♀ is little and doesn't like to fight, but it should not be underestimated. Its body is covered in poisonous barbs, and the small horn on its forehead is toxic.

NIDORINA

Type: Poison
Height: 2' 07"
Weight: 44.1 lbs.

The gentle Nidorina protects itself with cries containing ultrasonic waves that confuse and bewilder attackers.

NIDOQUEEN

Type: Poison-Ground
Height: 4' 03"
Weight: 132.3 lbs.

Stiff scales like needles cover Nidoqueen's body. When guarding its nest, it can bristle up the scales so the needles point out toward any intruder.

NIDORAN ♂

Type: Poison
Height: 1' 04"
Weight: 15.4 lbs.

When Nidoran♂ lifts its large ears above the grass, it's listening for anything that could be a threat. Its poison barbs can be extended for protection.

NIDORINO

Type: Poison
Height: 2' 11"
Weight: 43.0 lbs.

The aggressive Nidorino attacks without warning if it senses something amiss in its surroundings. The horn on its forehead is extremely poisonous.

NIDOKING

Type: Poison-Ground
Height: 4' 07"
Weight: 136.7 lbs.

Nidoking's hide is as hard as stone, and its tail is strong enough to snap a tree trunk effortlessly. In addition, the long horn on its head is full of venom. Stay clear!

DEDENNE

Type: Electric-Fairy
Height: 0' 08"
Weight: 4.9 lbs.

Dedenne uses its whiskers like antennas to communicate over long distances using electrical waves. It can soak up electricity through its tail.

CHINGLING

Type: Psychic
Height: 0' 08"
Weight: 1.3 lbs.

When Chingling hops about, a small orb bounces around inside its mouth, producing a noise like the sound of bells. It uses high-pitched sounds to attack its opponents' hearing.

CHIMECHO

Type: Psychic
Height: 2' 00"
Weight: 2.2 lbs.

The top of Chimecho's head is a sucker that lets it hang from a ceiling or a tree branch. It's light enough to float on the wind.

MIME JR.

Type: Psychic-Fairy
Height: 2' 00"
Weight: 28.7 lbs.

To enthrall and confuse an attacker, Mime Jr. copies its movements. While the opponent is bewildered, it makes its escape.

MR. MIME

Type: Psychic-Fairy
Height: 4' 03"
Weight: 120.1 lbs.

When it mimes being stuck behind an invisible wall, Mr. Mime is actually creating a psychic barrier with its fingertips. This barrier protects it from attacks.

SOLOSIS

Type: Psychic
Height: 1' 00"
Weight: 2.2 lbs.

The special liquid that surrounds Solosis protects it from any harsh conditions. They communicate with telepathy.

DUOSION

Type: Psychic
Height: 2' 00"
Weight: 17.6 lbs.

Duosion's brain is divided into two, so sometimes it tries to do two different things at the same time. When the brains are thinking together, Duosion's psychic power is at its strongest.

REUNICLUS

Type: Psychic
Height: 3' 03"
Weight: 44.3 lbs.

Reuniclus shake hands with each other to create a network between their brains. Working together boosts their psychic power, and they can crush huge rocks with their minds.

WYNAUT

Type: Psychic
Height: 2' 00"
Weight: 30.9 lbs.

When it's time to sleep, a group of Wynaut find a cave and snuggle up close together. Sweet berries are their favorite food.

WOBBUFFET

Type: Psychic
Height: 4' 03"
Weight: 62.8 lbs.

Wobbuffet prefers to hide in dark places, where its black tail can't be seen, and avoids battle when possible. If another Pokémon attacks it first, it puffs up its body and strikes back.

ROGGENROLA

Type: Rock
Height: 1' 04"
Weight: 39.7 lbs.

Each Roggenrola has an energy core at its center. The intense pressure in their underground home has compressed their bodies into a steely toughness.

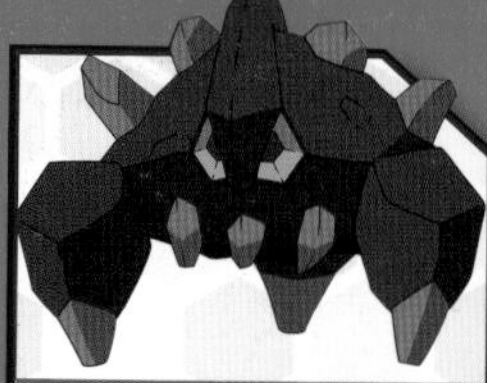

BOLDORE

Type: Rock
Height: 2' 11"
Weight: 224.9 lbs.

The energy within Boldore's body overflows, leaks out, and forms into orange crystals. Though its head always points in the same direction, it can quickly move sideways and backward.

GIGALITH

Type: Rock
Height: 5' 07"
Weight: 573.2 lbs.

After Gigalith soaks up the sun's rays, it uses its energy core to process that energy into a weapon. A blast of its compressed energy can destroy a mountain.

SABLEYE

Type: Dark-Ghost
Height: 1' 08"
Weight: 24.3 lbs.

Sableye lives in dark caves, where it digs up tasty gems to eat. Its gemstone eyes are influenced by its diet.

CARBINK

Type: Rock-Fairy
Height: 1' 00"
Weight: 12.6 lbs.

While excavating caves, miners and archeologists sometimes stumble upon Carbink sleeping deep underground. The stone on top of its head can fire beams of energy.

TAUROS

Type: Normal
Height: 4' 07"
Weight: 194.9 lbs.

To get pumped up for a fight, Tauros whips itself with its three tails. This is a sure sign that it's about to charge.

MILTANK

Type: Normal
Height: 3' 11
Weight: 166.4 lbs.

When Miltank spends time with babies, its milk becomes even more nourishing. Those who are ill or tired consume this nutritious milk to feel better.

MAREEP

Type: Electric
Height: 2' 00"
Weight: 17.2 lbs.

When static electricity builds up in Mareep's body, its soft coat puffs up to double its usual size. The fluffy wool helps regulate its temperature.

FLAAFFY

Type: Electric
Height: 2' 07"
Weight: 29.3 lbs.

Though Flaaffy's fluffy coat attracts electricity, it never has to worry about getting shocked, because its body is protected by rubbery skin. Its tail lights up when it's fully charged.

AMPHAROS

Type: Electric
Height: 4' 07"
Weight: 135.6 lbs.

Ampharos shines a bright light from the tip of its tail. Wandering travelers can see the light from far away and follow it to safety.

PINSIR

Type: Bug
Height: 4' 11"
Weight: 121.3 lbs.

Pinsir uses its long horns for both offense and defense. When it swings its head, the horns keep enemies at bay.

HERACROSS

Type: Bug-Fighting
Height: 4' 11"
Weight: 119.0 lbs.

Heracross is immensely strong. With its giant horn, it can throw an enemy much bigger than itself.

PACHIRISU

Type: Electric
Height: 1' 04"
Weight: 8.6 lbs.

When Pachirisu affectionately rub their cheeks together, they're sharing electric energy with each other. The balls of fur they shed crackle with static.

SLOWPOKE

Type: Water-Psychic
Height: 3' 11"
Weight: 79.4 lbs.

Slowpoke uses its tail for fishing, but it's often too distracted to notice when it gets a bite. No one knows what it daydreams about all day long.

SLOWBRO

Type: Water-Psychic
Height: 5' 03"
Weight: 173.1 lbs.

Apparently, Slowbro's tail is very tasty, so the biting Shellder will never let go.

SLOWKING

Type: Water-Psychic
Height: 6' 07"
Weight: 175.3 lbs.

Being bitten in the head had the unusual effect of focusing Slowking's mind. Its intelligence and intuition are impressive.

EXEGGCUTE

Type: Grass-Psychic
Height: 1' 04"
Weight: 5.5 lbs.

The six eggs that make up Exeggcute's body can be separated from one another, but thanks to their telepathic communication, they can find each other again quickly.

EXEGGUTOR

Type: Grass-Psychic
Height: 6' 07"
Weight: 264.6 lbs.

Although Exeggutor's three heads have minds of their own, they get along quite well. It's known as the "Walking Jungle."

CHATOT

Type: Normal-Flying
Height: 1' 08"
Weight: 4.2 lbs.

Chatot can mimic other Pokémon's cries and even human speech. A group of them will often pick up the same phrase and keep repeating it among themselves.

MANTYKE

Type: Water-Flying
Height: 3' 03"
Weight: 143.3 lbs.

Mantyke that live in different regions have different patterns on their backs. They're often found in the company of Remoraid.

MANTINE

Type: Water-Flying
Height: 6' 11"
Weight: 485.0 lbs.

An elegant and speedy swimmer, Mantine can gain enough momentum to launch itself out of the water and fly for hundreds of feet before splashing down again.

CLAMPERL

Type: Water
Height: 1' 04"
Weight: 115.7 lbs.

The glorious pearl it produces can be used as a focus for mystical powers. Over its lifetime, a Clamperl will only create a single pearl.

HUNTAIL

Type: Water
Height: 5' 07"
Weight: 59.5 lbs.

Huntail lives in the depths of the ocean, where it's always dark. Its lighted tail, which resembles a small creature, sometimes tricks others into attacking.

GOREBYSS

Type: Water
Height: 5' 11"
Weight: 49.8 lbs.

Gorebyss heralds the arrival of spring by turning even more vividly pink. Its long, thin mouth can reach into crevices in the rocky seafloor to eat the seaweed that grows there.

REMORAID

Type: Water
Height: 2' 00"
Weight: 26.5 lbs.

Remoraid is a master marksman, using sprays of water to shoot down moving targets hundreds of feet away. It often attaches itself to a Mantine in hopes of sharing a meal.

OCTILLERY

Type: Water
Height: 2' 11"
Weight: 62.8 lbs.

Octillery doesn't like being out in the open. It hides itself among craggy rocks, where it can spray ink to keep enemies away without revealing itself.

CORSOLA

Type: Water-Rock
Height: 2' 00"
Weight: 11.0 lbs.

Corsola is constantly shedding coral from its body as it grows. In polluted water, its branches become discolored.

CHINCHOU

Type: Water-Electric
Height: 1' 08"
Weight: 26.5 lbs.

Chinchou live deep in the ocean, where they flash the lights on their antennae to communicate. They can also pass electricity between their antennas.

LANTURN

Type: Water-Electric
Height: 3' 11"
Weight: 49.6 lbs.

Even in the dark depths of the ocean, Lanturn's light can be seen from a great distance. Because of this, it's known as "The Deep-Sea Star."

ALOMOMOLA

Type: Water
Height: 3' 11"
Weight: 69.7 lbs.

When Alomomola finds injured Pokémon in the open sea where it lives, it gently wraps its healing fins around them and guides them to shore.

LAPRAS

Type: Water-Ice
Height: 8' 02"
Weight: 485.0 lbs.

Gentle and intelligent, Lapras are happy to carry travelers across the water on their sturdy backs. Because they are easily caught, wild Lapras are growing more rare.

MOLTRES

Type: Fire-Flying
Height: 6' 07"
Weight: 132.3 lbs.

It is said that when Moltres appears, spring is not far behind. This Legendary Pokémon gives off flames as it flaps its wings.

ARTICUNO

Type: Ice-Flying
Height: 5' 07"
Weight: 122.1 lbs.

It is said that doomed travelers sometimes see Articuno in the mountains. This Legendary Pokémon can freeze water vapor in the air.

ZAPDOS

Type: Electric-Flying
Height: 5' 03"
Weight: 116.0 lbs.

It is said that Zapdos lives in thunderclouds. This Legendary Pokémon can control lightning and fling bolts at the ground.

BATTLE MOVE MATCH

Ash's first Kalos Gym Battle takes place at Santalune City's Gym against the awesome Gym Leader, Viola. It's a battle using two Pokémon each.
Ash starts out with Pikachu, while Viola uses Surskit. Surskit gains the upper hand, so Ash puts Fletchling into the battle arena. Fletchling defeats Surskit, so Viola brings out Vivillon, who successfully brings the challenge to an end. Ash is not happy. He challenges Viola to a rematch.
Look out for their next battle! In the meantime, match the battling Pokémon to their awesome moves.

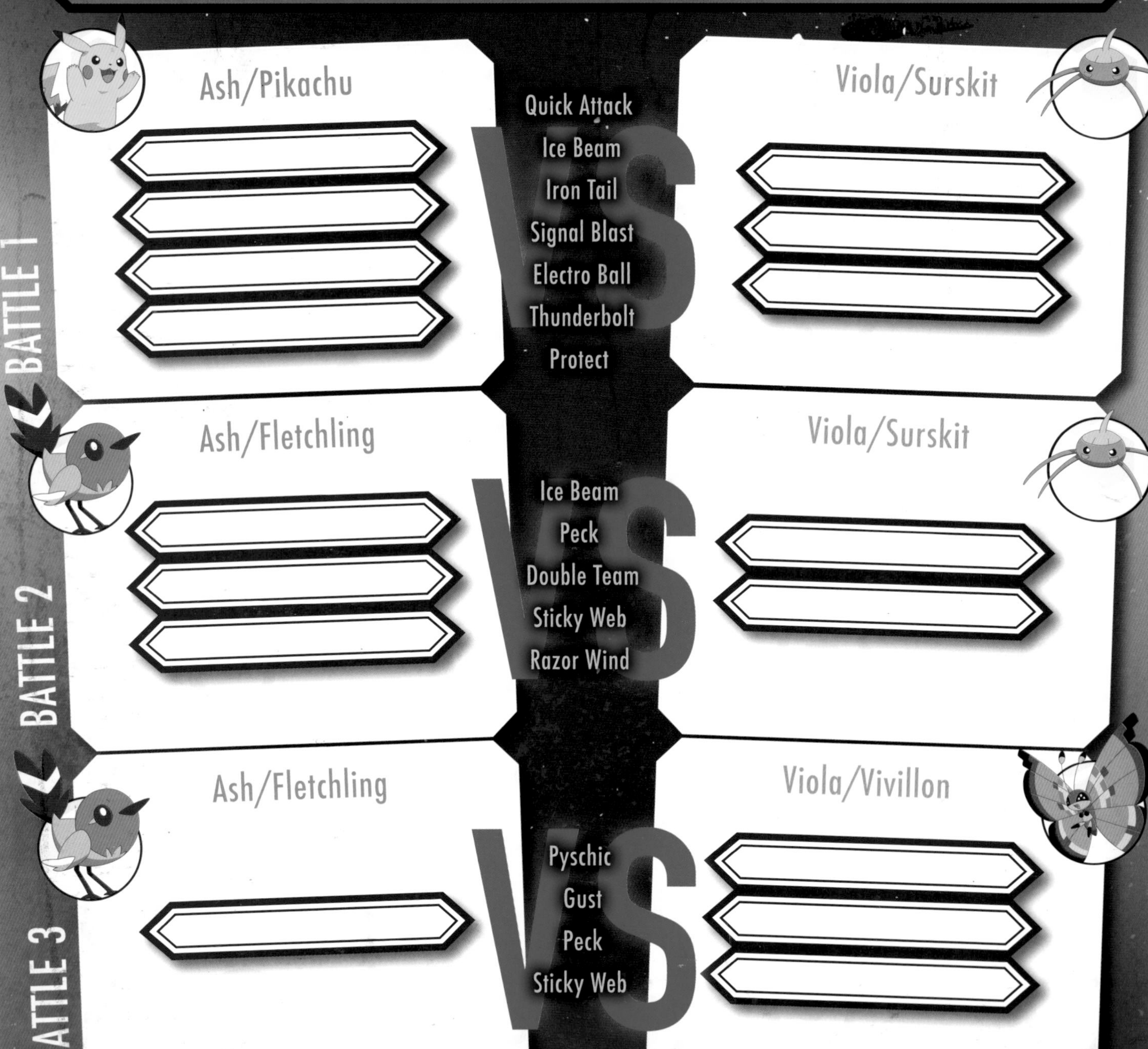

HOSTLY COPY CHALLENGE

the Ghost- and Poison-type Pokémon, stalks the shadows
t, absorbing heat and creating a creepy chill in the
udden shiver could mean a Gengar is hiding
! Before this ghostly creature creeps up on
arefully copy each part of this shadowy
non into the grid below.

Watch out, there's a chill in the air!

X Y

SHADOW PLAY

Ash is always looking for new Pokémon to add to his collection. There are lots of new species of Pokémon in the Kalos region. Help Ash check his Pokédex to find out which Pokémon are hiding in the shadows.

If you need a little extra help lighting up these secret shadows, un-jumble these Pokémon names.

1 KAMAZALA (Psychic type)

3 TOPLEEHILI (Electric-Normal type)

5 FLATMONFEL (Fire-Flying type)

2 SUBLASBURA (Grass-Poison type)

4 NASCELAME (Dragon-Flying type)

6 ROOPAVEN (Water type)

BATTLING ON THIN ICE!

After losing his first Gym Battle to Viola, the Gym Leader of Santalune City, Ash is more determined than ever to win the rematch and earn his first Kalos Gym Badge.

Fletchling and Pikachu are fully recovered, and Ash is putting them through some vigorous training, assisted by Alexa and her Pokémon, Noivern. He's really worried about how his Pokémon can overcome Vivillon's Gust and Surskit's Ice Beam and Sticky Web.

Ash still doesn't remember Serena from Professor Oak's Pokémon summer camp, but she's told him not to worry. For now, he needs to concentrate on his training . . .

"You were awesome, Ash!" Serena sighed. "Come on. I remember what you said when we met at summer camp—you never give up!"

"Thanks, Serena. You're a big help!" Ash laughed. "You're right. I'm NOT giving up. That just wouldn't be me at all."

"Come on then, Ash!" said Alexa. "Are you ready to go again?"

Alexa instructed her Noivern to blast Fletchling and Pikachu with Gust. The training was paying off because both Pokémon were able to stand their ground.

"Awesome! Looking good, you two!" shouted Ash. "Thanks, Alexa. That was some really helpful training!"

"Save your thanks until after you defeat my sister and win your first Kalos Gym badge!" Alexa laughed.

"Now all we need to figure out is how to deal with the ice battlefield and the Sticky Web," sighed Ash.

"Well, I can help you with the Sticky Web," said Clemont. "With the very best of my scientific skills!"

The friends all looked at one another and smiled. Clemont was a genius inventor, but sometimes his gadgets didn't quite work how they were supposed to.

"I call it . . ." Clemont announced proudly, ". . . the Sticky Web Sticky-Wicket Wasker Wonk! It replicates the stickiness of the the Sticky Web exactly."

"Wow! Science is amazing!" said Ash. "Let's try it out. Pikachu, Fletchling, get ready."

Clemont switched on his machine and locked it on his targets—the two Pokémon. *FIRE!*

Sticky Webs flew out of the machine, and Pikachu and Fletchling dived out of their way.

"Fantastic! Well done, you two," shouted Ash.

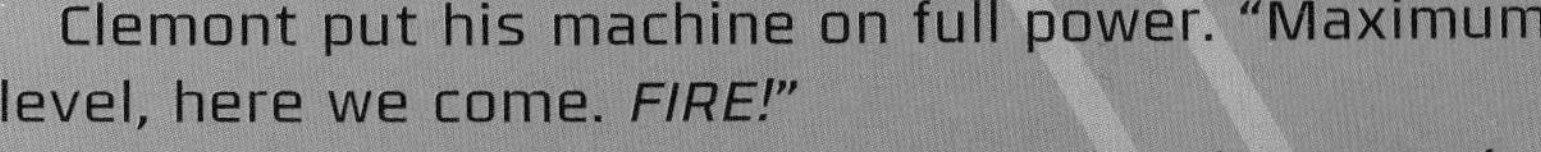

Clemont put his machine on full power. "Maximum level, here we come. *FIRE!*"

But nothing happened . . . until suddenly, *BOOM!* The machine exploded in a ball of fire.

"Oh, that shouldn't have happened . . ." groaned Clemont. The others smiled at him.

"Never mind, I've got another idea," cried Ash. "Let's use Froakie's special Frubbles to practice—they're like Sticky Web."

Pikachu and Fletchling successfully dodged Froakie's Frubbles.

"Well done, everybody! I think we're ready, guys. Thank you for all your help. Let's call it a day," said Ash sleepily.

Early the next day, Viola and Ash stood facing each other across the battle arena.

"So, Ash," said Viola, "my sister told me you were training hard yesterday. I'm looking forward to this!"

"Yeah, me too. Because this time I'm gonna win a badge!" Ash replied.

"Battle . . . begin!" called the referee.

Viola immediately directed Surskit to use Sticky Web.

But this time, Pikachu was ready.

With amazing skill, the little Electric Pokémon dodged and ducked and dived. Not one Sticky Web hit its target.

"Wow! That's fast!" cried Viola as Pikachu launched Thunderbolt.

Surskit countered with a Signal Beam.

Pikachu attacked with Iron Tail.

"Okay, time to refocus," cried Viola. Pikachu seemed to be gaining the upper hand.

Surskit froze the battlefield with an Ice Beam. Pikachu slipped on the icy surface.

"Get up, Pikachu," shouted Ash. "You can do it!"

Ash instructed Pikachu to dig in with Iron Tail and then use Thunderbolt. In a sizzling flash of light and electricity, Surskit dropped to the ground.

"Surskit is unable to battle. Pikachu wins!" shouted the referee.

Clemont, Bonnie, and Serena whooped with delight! Ash and Pikachu were on fire with their battle moves!

Ash grinned. "I choose Fletchling. Pikachu, return! Fletchling wants a chance for a rematch against Vivillon."

"Picture-perfect!" cried Viola. "Let's do this. Go, Vivillon!"

In a flurry of wings, Fletchling and Vivillon flew at each other. This was going to be a tough battle. The colorful Vivillon countered Fletchling's Steel Wing with Pyschic, followed by Gust, as Fletchling used Peck.

Fletchling seemed to be holding its own, when suddenly, Viola changed tactics and instructed Vivillon to use Sleep Powder.

Ash looked on in horror as Fletchling dropped to the ground, fast asleep, and Vivillon launched its final move—Solar Beam.

"Oh, no!" cried Ash. "Fletchling!" The little Flying-type Pokémon didn't move.

"Fletchling is unable to battle. Vivillon wins!" shouted the referee.

Ash's face fell.

"Come on, Ash!" cheered his friends. "Don't give up! We believe in you!"

"Well, you know there's no way my sister would let Ash win without a proper fight!" said Alexa, smiling at her sister.

"Pikachu, I need you to get back in there!" said Ash, more determined than ever to win the battle.

Vivillon launched a ferocious Gust. How was battle-weary Pikachu going to be able to withstand the powerful force?

"Ha, Pikachu can't beat my Vivillon in that state," Viola shouted.

"Yeah, well, there's no way we're giving up!" replied Ash. "We'll keep battling right up until the very end!"

Viola grinned. "I admire your persistence. But this *is* the end! Vivillon, Gust one more time!"

Using its last strength, Pikachu dug in its Iron Tail.

"Wow, that is so cool!" cried Bonnie from the sidelines. "Come on, Pikachu!"

The next few moments of the battle were a blur as the two Pokémon attacked with their classic moves—Solar Beam and Thunderbolt.

In a final attempt to win the battle, Viola instructed Vivillon to use Sleeping Powder, followed by a blast of Solar Beam.

Pikachu started to fall asleep. Was this the end of the battle?

"Pikachu, don't give in to it!" shouted Ash. "Use Electro Ball on yourself."

The air crackled with the force of the electricity. With a jerk, Pikachu shocked himself awake!

Clemont, Bonnie, and Serena were going crazy on the sidelines. They had never seen anything like it.

Viola paused mid-command, in surprise, as the valiant Pikachu fired his final shot—another Electro Ball. She wasn't quite quick enough to get Vivillon to use Solar Beam.

The blast of the Electro Ball

hit Vivillon full on. Suddenly, it started flying in a strange way.

"Look!" cried Clemont. "Vivillon's wing is covered in ice. It can't fly!"

Vivillon dropped to the ground, stunned. Viola ran towards it. "No! Vivillon!" she shouted.

"Vivillon is unable to battle. Pikachu wins!" called the referee. "Which means the winner of the match is . . . Ash!"

Ash grabbed Pikachu and sang out, "We did it, Pikachu!"

"Ash, that was amazing!" said Serena. The friends all huddled around Ash and Pikachu as Viola and Alexa walked over to the happy group.

"I couldn't have done it without all of you guys," said Ash.

"Congratulations, Ash," said Viola, as she handed Ash a Gym Badge. "This is to prove you won your Gym Battle against me!"

"Wow! The Bug Badge. Thank you, so much." Ash couldn't stop smiling.

"There are some things you can only see when looking through a camera's viewfinder. And things you'll only see clearly by living together with Pokémon," said Viola. "Keep strengthening the bonds you share with your Pokémon, and good luck!"

Ash couldn't have wished for a better day. He'd set out to win, and here he was with his first Kalos Gym Badge! Next stop, Cyllage City, to fight his second Gym Battle.

As Ash and his friends waved good-bye to Viola and Alexa, Ash turned to Serena. "So, Serena, where are you headed off to from here?"

Serena looked surprised. She smiled. "Uh? Me? I don't know . . . ?"

Ash looked at Clemont and Bonnie and then smiled shyly at Serena.

"Well . . ." he stuttered. "If you've got nothing better to do, why don't you join us?"

"Oh, cool!" said Bonnie.

"Thanks, guys!" Serena grinned. "Let me just sort out things with my mother . . . then Kalos adventure, here we come!"

TO BE CONTINUED ··································

KALOS TRAVELING PALS

When Clemont, Bonnie, and Serena said they would join Ash and Pikachu on their adventures in Kalos, Ash was very happy to welcome his new friends.

Grab your pens and pencils and color this cool picture of the new Pokémon pals!

KALOS COASTAL POKÉMON PATTERNS

Ash and his friends are having fun spotting new Kalos Coastal Pokémon on their journey through the region. Look at all the coastal Pokémon they've spotted so far. Complete each Pokémon pattern by drawing in the correct missing creature. Which Kalos Coastal Pokémon is your favorite so far? You can check them out in your Coastal Pokémon Pokédex.

DIGLETT

Type: Ground
Height: 0' 08"
Weight: 1.8 lbs.

Diglett live underground to protect their thin skin from the light. They come within a few feet of the surface to munch on the roots of plants.

DUGTRIO

Type: Ground
Height: 2' 04"
Weight: 73.4 lbs.

During battles, Dugtrio uses its impressive burrowing skill to its advantage, striking from below where the opponent can't see. No matter how hard the ground is, it can dig through.

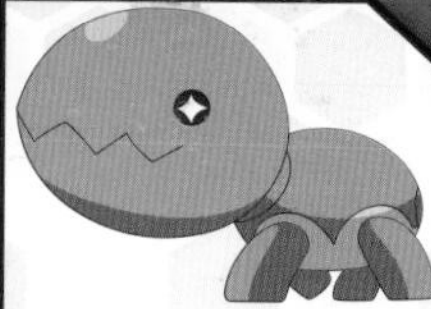

TRAPINCH

Type: Ground
Height: 2' 04"
Weight: 33.1 lbs.

Trapinch dig cone-shaped pits in the sand of their desert home. When something falls into the pit, they attack.

VIBRAVA

Type: Ground-Dragon
Height: 3' 07"
Weight: 33.7 lbs.

Vibrava produces ultrasonic waves by rubbing its wings together in a rapid motion. These waves can cause an intense headache.

FLYGON

Type: Ground-Dragon
Height: 6' 07"
Weight: 180.8 lbs.

When it needs a hiding place, Flygon beats its wings rapidly to create a sandstorm. This Pokémon is known as the "Desert Spirit."

GIBLE

Type: Dragon-Ground
Height: 2' 04"
Weight: 45.2 lbs.

Gible dig holes in the walls of warm caves to make their nests. Don't get too close, or they might pounce!

GABITE

Type: Dragon-Ground
Height: 4' 07"
Weight: 123.5 lbs.

While digging to expand its nest, Gabite sometimes finds sparkly gems that then become part of its hoard.

GARCHOMP

Type: Dragon-Ground
Height: 6' 03"
Weight: 209.4 lbs.

Garchomp can fly faster than the speed of sound. When it assumes a streamlined position for flight, it looks like a fighter jet.

GEODUDE

Type: Rock-Ground
Height: 1' 04"
Weight: 44.1 lbs.

Geodude look just like rocks when they aren't moving. They hold contests to see which one has the hardest surface by crashing into each other.

GRAVELER

Type: Rock-Ground
Height: 3' 03"
Weight: 231.5 lbs.

Graveler move by rolling downhill. They'll roll right over anything that gets in their way, and they don't even notice if bits of themselves break off in the process.

GOLEM

Type: Rock-Ground
Height: 4' 07"
Weight: 661.4 lbs.

When Golem roll down mountains, they leave deep grooves in the rock. Their boulder-like surface protects them from anything, even a dynamite blast.

SLUGMA

Type: Fire
Height: 2' 04"
Weight: 77.2 lbs.

In areas of volcanic activity, Slugma are regularly seen. They have to keep moving in search of heat, or the magma that makes up their bodies will harden.

MAGCARGO

Type: Fire-Rock
Height: 2' 07"
Weight: 121.3 lbs.

Magcargo's body is so hot that its brittle shell sometimes bursts into flame, giving off waves of intense heat.

SHUCKLE

Type: Bug-Rock
Height: 2' 00"
Weight: 45.2 lbs.

Shuckle keeps berries in its shell to eat them later. If it forgets, its movements eventually turn the berries into juice.

SKORUPI

Type: Poison-Bug
Height: 2' 07"
Weight: 26.5 lbs.

After burying itself in the sand, Skorupi lurks in hiding. If an intruder gets too close, it latches on with the poisonous claws on its tail.

DRAPION

Type: Poison-Dark
Height: 4' 03"
Weight: 135.6 lbs.

Drapion's strong arms could tear a car into scrap metal. The claws on its arms and tail are extremely toxic.

WOOPER

Type: Water-Ground
Height: 1' 04"
Weight: 18.7 lbs.

When the sun is out, Wooper stay in the water to keep cool. They go ashore at night, after the temperature drops, to look for food.

QUAGSIRE

Type: Water-Ground
Height: 4' 07"
Weight: 165.3 lbs.

The laid-back Quagsire often bumps into boats as it swims slowly through the river. Sometimes it lounges on the riverbed and waits for food to float by.

GOOMY

Type: Dragon
Height: 1' 00"
Weight: 6.2 lbs.

The slippery membrane that covers Goomy's body deflects the fists and feet of its attackers. To keep itself from drying out, it stays away from the sun.

SLIGGOO

Type: Dragon
Height: 2' 07"
Weight: 38.6 lbs.

The four horns on Sliggoo's head are sense organs that allow the Pokémon to find its way by sound and smell.

GOODRA

Type: Dragon
Height: 6' 07"
Weight: 331.8 lbs.

The affectionate Goodra just loves to give its Trainer a big hug! Unfortunately, its hugs leave the recipient covered in goo.

KARRABLAST

Type: Bug
Height: 1' 08"
Weight: 13.0 lbs.

Karrablast often attack Shelmet, trying to steal their shells. When electrical energy envelops them at the same time, they both evolve.

ESCAVALIER

Type: Bug-Steel
Height: 3' 03"
Weight: 72.8 lbs.

The stolen Shelmet shell protects Escavalier's body like armor. It uses its double lances to attack.

SHELMET

Type: Bug
Height: 1' 04"
Weight: 17.0 lbs.

Shelmet evolves when exposed to electricity, but only if Karrablast is nearby. It's unclear why this is the case.

ACCELGOR

Type: Bug
Height: 2' 07"
Weight: 55.8 lbs.

After coming out of its shell, Accelgor is light and quick, moving with the speed of a ninja. It wraps its body up to keep from drying out.

BELLSPROUT

Type: Grass-Poison
Height: 2' 04"
Weight: 8.8 lbs.

Bellsprout's flower resembles a face. Its stalklike body can move at unexpected speeds when it's chasing something.

WEEPINBELL

Type: Grass-Poison
Height: 3' 03"
Weight: 14.1 lbs.

With its sharp-edged leaves, Weepinbell slashes at its opponents. The fluid it spits is extremely acidic.

VICTREEBEL

Type: Grass-Poison
Height: 5' 07"
Weight: 34.2 lbs.

Explorers have gone in search of the large colonies of Victreebel rumored to exist deep in the jungle, but they disappeared without a trace.

CARNIVINE

Type: Grass
Height: 4' 07"
Weight: 59.5 lbs.

Carnivine wraps itself around trees in swampy areas. It gives off a sweet aroma that lures others close, then attacks.

GASTLY

Type: Ghost-Poison
Height: 4' 03"
Weight: 0.2 lbs.

Gastly's body is formed of poisonous gases. It can envelop opponents in its gaseous body to cut off their air.

HAUNTER

Type: Ghost-Poison
Height: 5' 03"
Weight: 0.2 lbs.

Haunter lurks in dark places, waiting for people to pass by so it can steal their life force with a ghostly lick.

GENGAR

Type: Ghost-Poison
Height: 4' 11"
Weight: 89.3 lbs.

Gengar stalks the shadows at night, absorbing heat and creating a creepy chill in the air. A sudden shiver could mean a Gengar is hiding nearby.

POLIWAG

Type: Water
Height: 2' 00"
Weight: 27.3 lbs.

The direction of the spiral pattern on Poliwag's belly is different depending on where it lives. It can get around much more easily in the water than on land.

POLIWHIRL

Type: Water
Height: 3' 03"
Weight: 44.1 lbs.

Poliwhirl sweats profusely when on land to keep its skin moist. Though its legs have developed to make walking easier, it prefers to swim.

POLIWRATH

Type: Water-Fighting
Height: 4' 03"
Weight: 119.0 lbs.

A strong and tireless swimmer, Poliwrath is tough enough to withstand the constant waves and currents of the ocean.

POLITOED

Type: Water
Height: 3' 07"
Weight: 74.7 lbs.

It sounds an echoing cry to summon Poliwag and Poliwhirl from anywhere within earshot. When more than two Politoed gather together, they join voices in a bellowing song.

EKANS

Type: Poison
Height: 6' 07"
Weight: 15.2 lbs.

You can tell how old an Ekans is by the length of its body, because it keeps growing year after year. It coils up around a branch to sleep at night.

ARBOK

Type: Poison
Height: 11' 06"
Weight: 143.3 lbs.

When threatened, Arbok flares its hood to expose its belly pattern, which looks like a scary face. This is often enough to make enemies run away.

STUNFISK

Type: Ground-Electric
Height: 2' 04"
Weight: 24.3 lbs.

Stunfisk buries its flat body in mud, so it's hard to see and often gets stepped on. When that happens, its thick skin keeps it from being hurt, and it zaps the offender with a cheery smile.

BARBOACH

Type: Water-Ground
Height: 1' 04"
Weight: 4.2 lbs.

Barboach is covered in a slippery slime, so it's difficult for an opponent to get a good grip. It uses its whiskers to sense its surroundings in places where the water isn't clear.

WHISCASH

Type: Water-Ground
Height: 2' 11"
Weight: 52.0 lbs.

Whiscash lives at the bottom of a swamp and claims the entire swamp as its territory. It thrashes wildly to startle approaching enemies.

PURRLOIN

Type: Dark
Height: 1' 04"
Weight: 22.3 lbs.

Purrloin acts cute and innocent to trick people into trusting it. Then it steals their stuff.

LIEPARD

Type: Dark
Height: 3' 07"
Weight: 82.7 lbs.

Elegant and swift, Liepard can move through the night without a sound. It uses this stealth to execute sneak attacks.

POOCHYENA

Type: Dark
Height: 1' 08"
Weight: 30.0 lbs.

An unrelenting tracker, Poochyena can use scent to stay on the trail of a fleeing opponent long after it disappears from view.

MIGHTYENA

Type: Dark
Height: 3' 03"
Weight: 81.6 lbs.

In the wild, Mightyena hunt in packs and work together to take down an opponent. Skilled Trainers find that this ancient instinct makes them obedient partners.

PATRAT

Type: Normal
Height: 1' 08"
Weight: 25.6 lbs.

Wary and cautious, Patrat are very serious about their job as lookouts. They store food in their cheeks so they don't have to leave their post.

WATCHOG

Type: Normal
Height: 3' 07"
Weight: 59.5 lbs.

Watchog can make its stripes and eyes glow in the dark. Its tail stands straight up to alert others when it spots an intruder.

PAWNIARD

Type: Dark-Steel
Height: 1' 08"
Weight: 22.5 lbs.

Pawniard's body is covered in blades, which it keeps sharp by polishing them after battle. Even when hurt, it's a relentless hunter.

BISHARP

Type: Dark-Steel
Height: 5' 03"
Weight: 154.3 lbs.

When Pawniard hunt in a pack, Bisharp leads them and gives the orders. It's often the one that deals the final blow.

KLEFKI

Type: Steel-Fairy
Height: 0' 08"
Weight: 6.6 lbs.

To keep valuables locked up tight, give the key to a Klefki. This Pokémon loves to collect keys, and it will guard its collection with all its might.

MURKROW

Type: Dark-Flying
Height: 1' 08"
Weight: 4.6 lbs.

Some people believe that if you see a Murkrow at night, bad luck will follow. This Pokémon is attracted to shiny objects and often swipes them to add to its hoard.

HONCHKROW

Type: Dark-Flying
Height: 2' 11"
Weight: 60.2 lbs.

When Honchkrow cries out in its deep voice, several Murkrow will appear to answer the call. It's most active after dark.

FOONGUS

Type: Grass-Poison
Height: 0' 08"
Weight: 2.2 lbs.

Foongus uses its deceptive Poké Ball pattern to lure people or Pokémon close. Then, it attacks with poison spores.

AMOONGUSS

Type: Grass-Poison
Height: 2' 00"
Weight: 23.1 lbs.

In a swaying dance, Amoonguss waves its arm caps, which look like Poké Balls, in an attempt to lure the unwary. It doesn't often work.

LOTAD

Type: Water-Grass
Height: 1' 08"
Weight: 5.7 lbs.

The large, flat leaf on Lotad's back makes an excellent ferry for smaller Pokémon that need to cross water.

LOMBRE

Type: Water-Grass
Height: 3' 11"
Weight: 71.6 lbs.

When Lombre spots someone fishing from the sunny shores where it makes its home, it often gives the line a playful tug.

LUDICOLO

Type: Water-Grass
Height: 4' 11"
Weight: 121.3 lbs.

Ludicolo just can't help leaping into a joyful dance when it hears a festive tune. Rhythmic music fills it with energy.

BUIZEL

Type: Water
Height: 2' 04"
Weight: 65.0 lbs.

Buizel rapidly spins its two tails to propel itself through the water. The flotation sac around its neck keeps its head up without effort, and it can deflate the sac to dive.

FLOATZEL

Type: Water
Height: 3' 07"
Weight: 73.9 lbs.

The flotation sac that surrounds its entire body makes Floatzel very good at rescuing people in the water. It can float them to safety like an inflatable raft.

BASCULIN

Type: Water
Height: 3' 03"
Weight: 39.7 lbs.

An ongoing feud exists between Basculin with blue stripes and Basculin with red stripes. Because they're constantly fighting, they are rarely found in the same place.

PHANTUMP

Type: Ghost-Grass
Height: 1' 04"
Weight: 15.4 lbs.

It is said that when the spirits of wandering children inhabit old tree stumps, these Pokémon are created. Phantump dwell in lonely forests, far away from people.

TREVENANT

Type: Ghost-Grass
Height: 4' 11"
Weight: 156.5 lbs.

Using its roots, Trevenant can control the trees around it to protect its forest home. Smaller Pokémon sometimes live in its hollow body.

PUMPKABOO

Type: Ghost-Grass
Height: 1' 04"
Weight: 11.0 lbs.

The nocturnal Pumpkaboo tends to get restless as darkness falls. Stories say it serves as a guide for wandering spirits, leading them through the night to find their true home.

GOURGEIST

Type: Ghost-Grass
Height: 2' 11"
Weight: 27.6 lbs.

During the new moon, the eerie song of the Gourgeist echoes through town, bringing woe to anyone who hears it.

LITWICK

Type: Ghost-Fire
Height: 1' 00"
Weight: 6.8 lbs.

Litwick pretends to guide people and Pokémon with its light, but following it is a bad idea. The ghostly flame absorbs life energy for use as fuel.

LAMPENT

Type: Ghost-Fire
Height: 2' 00"
Weight: 28.7 lbs.

Lampent tends to lurk grimly around hospitals, waiting for someone to take a bad turn so it can absorb the departing spirit. The stolen spirits keep its fire burning.

CHANDELURE

Type: Ghost-Fire
Height: 3' 03"
Weight: 75.6 lbs.

Chandelure's spooky flames can burn the spirit right out of someone. If that happens, the spirit becomes trapped in this world, endlessly wandering.

ROTOM

Type: Electric-Ghost
Height: 1' 00"
Weight: 0.7 lbs.

Scientists are conducting ongoing research on Rotom, which shows potential as a power source. Sometimes, it sneaks into electrical appliances and causes trouble.

MAGNEMITE

Type: Electric-Steel
Height: 1' 00"
Weight: 13.2 lbs.

From the units at its sides, Magnemite generates an antigravity field to keep itself afloat. The units can also unleash electrical attacks.

MAGNETON

Type: Electric-Steel
Height: 3' 03"
Weight: 132.3 lbs.

Several Magnemite link together to form a single Magneton. When Magneton is nearby, the magnetic waves it gives off jumble radio signals and raise the surrounding temperature.

MAGNEZONE

Type: Electric-Steel
Height: 3' 11"
Weight: 396.8 lbs.

Magnezone give off a strong magnetic field that they can't always control. Sometimes they attract each other by accident and stick so tightly that they have trouble separating.

VOLTORB

Type: Electric
Height: 1' 08"
Weight: 22.9 lbs.

Voltorb closely resembles a Poké Ball and often lurks around power plants. People who try to pick it up get zapped.

ELECTRODE

Type: Electric
Height: 3' 11"
Weight: 146.8 lbs.

The electricity it stores in its body often overflows. Because of its tendency to explode at the slightest provocation, Electrode is known as "The Bomb Ball."

TRUBBISH

Type: Poison
Height: 2' 00"
Weight: 68.3 lbs.

Trubbish live in grungy, germy, grimy places and release a gas that induces sleep in anyone who breathes it. They were created when household garbage reacted with chemical waste.

GARBODOR

Type: Poison
Height: 6' 03"
Weight: 236.6 lbs.

Garbodor wraps its long left arm around an opponent to bring it within range of its poisonous breath. It creates new kinds of poison by eating garbage.

SWINUB

Type: Ice-Ground
Height: 1' 04"
Weight: 14.3 lbs.

With its sensitive nose, Swinub can sniff out buried food or the source of a hot spring. If it catches an intriguing scent, it will rush off to track it down.

PILOSWINE

Type: Ice-Ground
Height: 3' 07"
Weight: 123.0 lbs.

Piloswine can't see very well because the long hair that protects it from the cold also covers its eyes. The rough surface of its hooves grips the ice to keep it from slipping.

MAMOSWINE

Type: Ice-Ground
Height: 8' 02"
Weight: 641.5 lbs.

Mamoswine have been around since the last ice age, but the warmer climate reduced their population. Their huge twin tusks are formed of ice.

BERGMITE

Type: Ice
Height: 3' 03"
Weight: 219.4 lbs.

When cracks form in Bergmite's icy body, it uses freezing air to patch itself up with new ice. It lives high in the mountains.

AVALUGG

Type: Ice
Height: 6' 07"
Weight: 1113.3 lbs.

Avalugg's broad, flat back is a common resting place for groups of Bergmite. Its big, bulky body can crush obstacles in its path.

CUBCHOO

Type: Ice
Height: 1' 08"
Weight: 18.7 lbs.

Even a healthy Cubchoo always has a runny nose. Its sniffles power its freezing attacks.

BEARTIC

Type: Ice
Height: 8' 06"
Weight: 573.2 lbs.

Beartic live in the far north, where the seas are very cold. Their fangs and claws are made of ice formed by their own freezing breath.

SMOOCHUM

Type: Ice-Psychic
Height: 1' 04"
Weight: 13.2 lbs.

When Smoochum encounters an unfamiliar object, it conducts an examination using its sensitive lips. Its memory of what it does and doesn't like is also stored in its lips.

JYNX

Type: Ice-Psychic
Height: 4' 07"
Weight: 89.5 lbs.

Jynx talk to each other in a complex language that resembles human speech. Researchers are still trying to figure out what they're saying.

VANILLITE

Type: Ice
Height: 1' 04"
Weight: 12.6 lbs.

When the sun rose and cast its light on icicles, Vanillite were created. With their icy breath, they can surround themselves with snow showers.

VANILLISH

Type: Ice
Height: 3' 07"
Weight: 90.4 lbs.

Vanillish live in snow-covered mountains and battle using particles of ice they create by chilling the air around them.

VANILLUXE

Type: Ice
Height: 4' 03"
Weight: 126.8 lbs.

From the water it gulps down, Vanilluxe creates snowy stormclouds inside its body. When it becomes angry, it uses those clouds to form a raging blizzard.

SNOVER

Type: Grass-Ice
Height: 3' 03"
Weight: 111.3 lbs.

Snover live high in the mountains most of the year, but in the winter, they migrate to lower elevations.

ABOMASNOW

Type: Grass-Ice
Height: 7' 03"
Weight: 298.7 lbs.

Snow-covered mountains are Abomasnow's preferred habitat. It creates blizzards to hide itself and keep others away.

DELIBIRD

Type: Ice-Flying
Height: 2' 11"
Weight: 35.3 lbs.

Delibird stores food bundled up in its tail, so it never goes hungry when it's traveling in the mountains. It happily shares food with anyone who needs rescuing.

SNEASEL

Type: Dark-Ice
Height: 2' 11"
Weight: 61.7 lbs.

Sneasel keeps its sharp, hook-like claws retracted inside its paws most of the time. When it's attacked, the claws spring out and rip at the aggressor.

WEAVILE

Type: Dark-Ice
Height: 3' 07"
Weight: 75.0 lbs.

In the snowy places where they live, Weavile communicate with others in the area by leaving carvings in tree trunks. They work together to hunt for food.

TIMBURR

Type: Fighting
Height: 2' 00"
Weight: 27.6 lbs.

Timburr always carries a wooden beam, which it trades for bigger ones as it grows. These Pokémon can be a big help to construction workers.

GURDURR

Type: Fighting
Height: 3' 11"
Weight: 88.2 lbs.

With its strong muscles, Gurdurr can wield its steel beam with ease in battle. It's so sturdy that a whole team of wrestlers couldn't knock it down.

CONKELDURR

Type: Fighting
Height: 4' 07"
Weight: 191.8 lbs.

Conkeldurr spin their concrete pillars to attack. It's said that long ago, people first learned about concrete from these Pokémon.

TORKOAL

Type: Fire
Height: 1' 08"
Weight: 177.2 lbs.

Torkoal often take up residence in abandoned coal mines. When threatened, they spew a cloud of black soot.

SANDSHREW

Type: Ground
Height: 2' 00"
Weight: 26.5 lbs.

Sandshrew can roll up into a ball to protect its soft belly. It lives underground in arid lands and doesn't like to get wet.

SANDSLASH

Type: Ground
Height: 3' 03"
Weight: 65.0 lbs.

When Sandslash rolls into a ball, the spikes on its back stick out in all directions. These spikes sometimes break off if it digs too fast, but they grow back quickly.

ARON

Type: Steel-Rock
Height: 1' 04"
Weight: 132.3 lbs.

When Aron can't find enough food in its mountain home, it might resort to chewing up railroad tracks.

LAIRON

Type: Steel-Rock
Height: 2' 11"
Weight: 264.6 lbs.

Lairon's favorite food is iron ore. In battles over territory, these Pokémon smash into each other with their steel bodies.

AGGRON

Type: Steel-Rock
Height: 6' 11"
Weight: 793.7 lbs.

With horns of steel, Aggron can dig tunnels through solid rock in search of iron ore to eat.

LARVITAR

Type: Rock-Ground
Height: 2' 00"
Weight: 158.7 lbs.

Larvitar uses soil as food, and its appetite is so great that it could eat an entire mountain. Afterward, it sleeps and grows.

PUPITAR

Type: Rock-Ground
Height: 3' 11"
Weight: 335.1 lbs.

Pupitar can pressurize gases inside its rock-hard shell and use them for propulsion.

TYRANITAR

Type: Rock-Dark
Height: 6' 07"
Weight: 445.3 lbs.

When Tyranitar goes on a rampage, it causes so much damage to the landscape that maps have to be updated.

HEATMOR

Type: Fire
Height: 4' 07"
Weight: 127.9 lbs.

Heatmor can control the flame from its mouth like a tongue, and the fire is so hot that it can melt through steel. Heatmor and Durant are natural enemies.

DURANT

Type: Bug-Steel
Height: 1' 00"
Weight: 72.8 lbs.

The heavily armored Durant work together to keep attackers away from their colony. Durant and Heatmor are natural enemies.

SPINARAK

Type: Bug-Poison
Height: 1' 08"
Weight: 18.7 lbs.

While waiting for prey to blunder into its sturdy web, the amazingly patient Spinarak can sit motionless for days at a time.

ARIADOS

Type: Bug-Poison
Height: 3' 07"
Weight: 73.9 lbs.

The web Ariados spins is made of thin silk, strong enough to bind and hold an enemy. The tiny hooks on its feet make it an excellent climber.

SPEAROW

Type: Normal-Flying
Height: 1' 00"
Weight: 4.4 lbs.

With its short wings, Spearow has to flap very quickly to stay in the air. It often looks for food hiding in the grass.

FEAROW

Type: Normal-Flying
Height: 3' 11"
Weight: 83.8 lbs.

Thanks to its impressive stamina, Fearow can fly for hours without stopping for a break. Its fearsome beak is used in battle.

CRYOGONAL

Type: Ice
Height: 3' 07"
Weight: 326.3 lbs.

Cryogonal's crystalline structure is made of ice formed in snow clouds. With its long chains of ice crystals, it unleashes a freezing attack.

SKARMORY

Type: Steel-Flying
Height: 5' 07"
Weight: 111.3 lbs.

Skarmory build their nests in thorny bushes, so their wings toughen up from an early age. The hard armor that covers them doesn't impair their flying speed.

NOIBAT

Type: Flying-Dragon
Height: 1' 08"
Weight: 17.6 lbs.

Noibat live in lightless caves and communicate with ultrasonic waves emitted from their ears. These waves can make a strong man dizzy.

NOIVERN

Type: Flying-Dragon
Height: 4' 11"
Weight: 187.4 lbs.

Noivern are masters when it comes to battling in the dark. The ultrasonic waves they release from their ears are powerful enough to crush a boulder.

GLIGAR

Type: Ground-Flying
Height: 3' 07"
Weight: 142.9 lbs.

Clinging to the side of a cliff, Gligar has the high ground—and the element of surprise. It strikes from above, grabbing onto its startled opponent's face.

GLISCOR

Type: Ground-Flying
Height: 6' 07"
Weight: 93.7 lbs.

Gliscor hangs upside-down from trees, watching for its chance to attack. At the right moment, it silently swoops, with its long tail ready to seize its opponent.

HOOTHOOT

Type: Normal-Flying
Height: 2' 04"
Weight: 46.7 lbs.

Although Hoothoot does have two feet, it's rare to see them both at the same time. Usually it balances on one foot while keeping the other tucked up into its feathers.

NOCTOWL

Type: Normal-Flying
Height: 5' 03"
Weight: 89.9 lbs.

Noctowl turns its head backward when it needs to concentrate. Its eyes are designed to focus the faintest light, so it can see in near-total darkness.

IGGLYBUFF

Type: Normal-Fairy
Height: 1' 00"
Weight: 2.2 lbs.

Igglybuff has very short legs, so instead of walking, it usually moves by bouncing. If it gets off-balance, it starts rolling and can't stop.

JIGGLYPUFF

Type: Normal-Fairy
Height: 1' 08"
Weight: 12.1 lbs.

Jigglypuff is known for its soothing lullabies. It can inflate its round body, which gives it enough air to keep singing until everyone falls asleep.

WIGGLYTUFF

Type: Normal-Fairy
Height: 3' 03"
Weight: 26.5 lbs.

An angry Wigglytuff may look much larger than normal, because it will suck in air to puff itself up. Their fur is incredibly soft and snuggly.

SHUPPET

Type: Ghost
Height: 2' 00"
Weight: 5.1 lbs.

Shuppet are drawn to unpleasant emotions. They sometimes lurk outside houses at night to feed on the inhabitants' bad vibes.

BANETTE

Type: Ghost
Height: 3' 07"
Weight: 27.6 lbs.

Banette used to be a child's plaything. When it was thrown out, it became a Pokémon out of spite toward its former owner.

ZORUA

Type: Dark
Height: 2' 04"
Weight: 27.6 lbs.

Zorua can use the power of illusion to make itself look like a person or a different Pokémon. It sometimes uses the resulting confusion to flee from a battle.

ZOROARK

Type: Dark
Height: 5' 03"
Weight: 178.8 lbs.

Masters of deception, Zoroark are able to create entire landscapes out of illusions. In this way, they can scare or trick people away from their territory and protect their pack.

GOTHITA

Type: Psychic
Height: 1' 04"
Weight: 12.8 lbs.

Gothita's wide eyes are always fixed on something. It seems when they stare like that, they're seeing what others cannot.

GOTHORITA

Type: Psychic
Height: 2' 04"
Weight: 39.7 lbs.

Gothorita draw their power from starlight. On starry nights, they can make stones float and control people's movements with their enhanced psychic power.

GOTHITELLE

Type: Psychic
Height: 4' 11"
Weight: 97.0 lbs.

Gothitelle observes the stars to predict the future. It sometimes distorts the air around itself to reveal faraway constellations.

BONSLY

Type: Rock
Height: 1' 08"
Weight: 33.1 lbs.

Bonsly prefers to live in dry places. When its body is storing excess moisture, it releases water from its eyes, making it look like it's crying.

SUDOWOODO

Type: Rock
Height: 3' 11"
Weight: 83.8 lbs.

For protection, Sudowoodo disguises itself as a tree, though its body seems to be more like a rock than like a plant. It dislikes water and will avoid rain if at all possible.

SPINDA

Type: Normal
Height: 3' 07"
Weight: 11.0 lbs.

Every Spinda's spot pattern is unique. They totter about in a haphazard fashion, which makes aiming at them very difficult.

TEDDIURSA

Type: Normal
Height: 2' 00"
Weight: 19.4 lbs.

Teddiursa hides food all over to prepare for the scarcity of winter. Its paws are soaked in honey, so it always has a snack.

URSARING

Type: Normal
Height: 5' 11"
Weight: 277.3 lbs.

Despite its size, Ursaring can climb to the very tops of trees to find food and a safe place to sleep. It can also sniff out tasty roots buried deep in the ground.

LICKITUNG

Type: Normal
Height: 3' 11"
Weight: 144.4 lbs.

Lickitung's sticky tongue is twice as long as its body. It uses this long, mobile tongue as an extra appendage.

LICKILICKY

Type: Normal
Height: 5' 07"
Weight: 308.6 lbs.

Lickilicky can make its long tongue even longer, stretching it out to wrap around food or foe. Its drool causes a lasting numbness.

SCYTHER

Type: Bug-Flying
Height: 4' 11"
Weight: 123.5 lbs.

With the razor-sharp scythes on its arms, Scyther can unleash slashing attacks faster than the eye can see.

SCIZOR

Type: Bug-Steel
Height: 5' 11"
Weight: 260.1 lbs.

Scizor's steely pincers can crush even the hardest objects. The eye patterns are meant to scare off enemies.

DITTO

Type: Normal
Height: 1' 00"
Weight: 8.8 lbs.

When Sandslash rolls into a ball, the spikes on its back stick out in all directions. These spikes sometimes break off if it digs too fast, but they grow back quickly.

SWABLU

Type: Normal-Flying
Height: 1' 04"
Weight: 2.6 lbs.

If a cottony Pokémon flutters out of the sky and lands lightly on your head, it's probably a Swablu pretending to be a hat. No one knows why it does this.

ALTARIA

Type: Dragon-Flying
Height: 3' 07"
Weight: 45.4 lbs.

In its lovely soprano voice, Altaria sings sweetly as it flies through sunny skies. It is often mistaken for a passing cloud.

DRUDDIGON

Type: Dragon
Height: 5' 03"
Weight: 306.4 lbs.

Druddigon can't move if it gets too cold, so it soaks up the sun with its wings. It can navigate tight caves at a brisk pace.

DEINO

Type: Dark-Dragon
Height: 2' 07"
Weight: 38.1 lbs.

Deino can't see, so they explore their surroundings by biting and crashing into things. Because of this, they are often covered in cuts and scratches.

ZWEILOUS

Type: Dark-Dragon
Height: 4' 07"
Weight: 110.2 lbs.

Zweilous has a ravenous appetite and exhausts the local food supply before moving on. Rather than working together, its two heads compete for food.

HYDREIGON

Type: Dark-Dragon
Height: 5' 11"
Weight: 352.7 lbs.

The smaller heads on Hydreigon's arms don't have brains, but they can still eat. Any movement within its line of sight will be greeted with a frightening attack.

DRATINI

Type: Dragon
Height: 5' 11"
Weight: 7.3 lbs.

Very few people have seen Dratini in the wild, so it's known as the "Mirage Pokémon." It sheds its skin several times a year as it grows.

DRAGONAIR

Type: Dragon
Height: 13' 01"
Weight: 36.4 lbs.

With the mystical orbs on its neck and tail, Dragonair is said to be able to control weather patterns.

DRAGONITE

Type: Dragon-Flying
Height: 7' 03"
Weight: 463.0 lbs.

Dragonite can fly around the whole world in less than a day. It lives far out at sea and comes to the aid of wrecked ships.

XERNEAS

Type: Fairy
Height: 9' 10"
Weight: 474.0 lbs.

Xerneas's horns shine in all the colors of the rainbow. It is said that this Legendary Pokémon can share the gift of endless life.

YVELTAL

Type: Dark-Flying
Height: 19' 00"
Weight: 447.5 lbs.

When Yveltal spreads its dark wings, its feathers give off a red glow. It is said that this Legendary Pokémon can absorb the life energy of others.

ZYGARDE

Type: Dragon-Ground
Height: 16' 05"
Weight: 672.4 lbs.

Zygarde dwells deep within a cave in the Kalos region. It is said that this Legendary Pokémon is a guardian of the ecosystem.

MEWTWO

Type: Psychic
Height: 6' 07"
Weight: 269.0 lbs.

This incredibly powerful Pokémon was created as part of a brutal scientific experiment involving genetic splicing. As a result, Mewtwo is extremely savage and dangerous.

MEGA EVOLUTION POKÉDEX

MEGA GYARADOS
Height: 21' 04" Weight: 672.4 lbs.

On their journey through the Kalos region, Ash and his friends meet Professor Sycamore. He is a scientist at the forefront of groundbreaking research on Pokémon Evolution, and through him Ash discovers the secrets of Mega Evolution.

A Pokémon can only evolve to its Mega form during battle. Once the battle ends, the Mega-Evolved Pokémon will return to its usual state. During the Mega Evolution process, some Pokémon may change their abilities or even their Pokémon type.

MEGA VENUSAUR
Height: 7' 10"
Weight: 342.8 lbs.

MEGA CHARIZARD X
Height: 5' 07"
Weight: 243.6 lbs.

MEGA MEDICHAM
Height: 4' 03"
Weight: 69.4 lbs.

MEGA ABSOL
Height: 3' 11"
Weight: 108.0 lbs.

MEGA MAWILE

Height: 3' 03" Weight: 51.8 lbs.

MEGA AERODACTYL

Height: 6' 11" Weight: 174.2 lbs.

MEGA MANECTRIC

Height: 5' 11" Weight: 97.0 lbs.

MEGA HOUNDOOM

Height: 6' 03" Weight: 109.1 lbs.

MEGA AMPHAROS

Height: 4' 07" Weight: 135.6 lbs.

MEGA PINSIR

Height: 5' 07" Weight: 130.1 lbs.

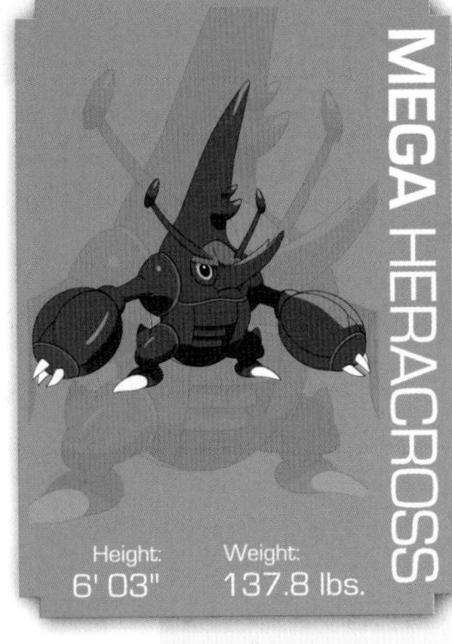

MEGA HERACROSS

Height: 6' 03" Weight: 137.8 lbs.

MEGA GARCHOMP

Height: 6' 03" Weight: 209.4 lbs.

MEGA GENGAR

Height: 4' 07" Weight: 89.3 lbs.

MEGA ABOMASNOW

Height: 8' 10" Weight: 407.9 lbs.

MEGA AGGRON

Height: 7' 03" Weight: 870.8 lbs.

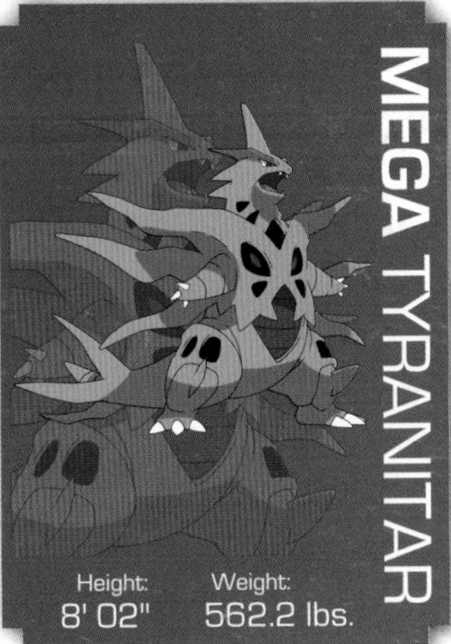

MEGA TYRANITAR

Height: 8' 02" Weight: 562.2 lbs.

MEGA BANETTE

Height: 3' 11" Weight: 28.7 lbs.

MEGA SCIZOR

Height: 6' 07" Weight: 275.6 lbs.

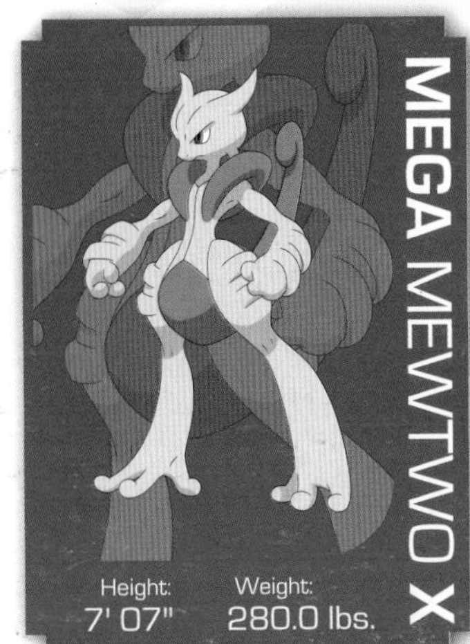

MEGA MEWTWO **X**

Height: 7' 07" Weight: 280.0 lbs.

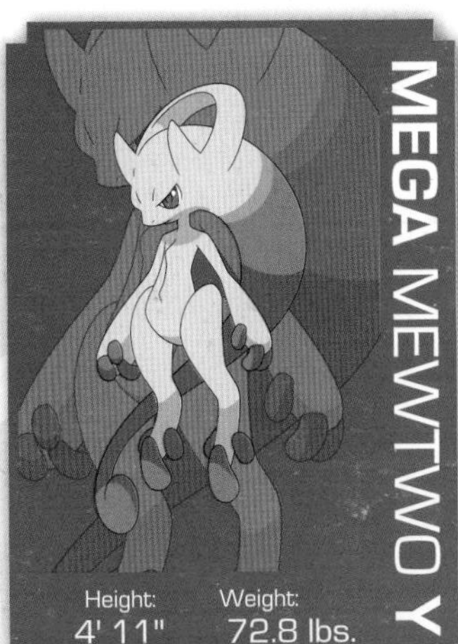

MEGA MEWTWO **Y**

Height: 4' 11" Weight: 72.8 lbs.

SERENA'S FIRST POKÉMON

Serena has arrived at Professor Sycamore's research lab to choose her first Pokémon. Who will she pick—Chespin, Fennekin, or Froakie? Using the Pokémon key below, help Serena work her way through the lab so she can choose her First Pokémon.

RIGHT

LEFT

UP

DOWN

START

FINISH

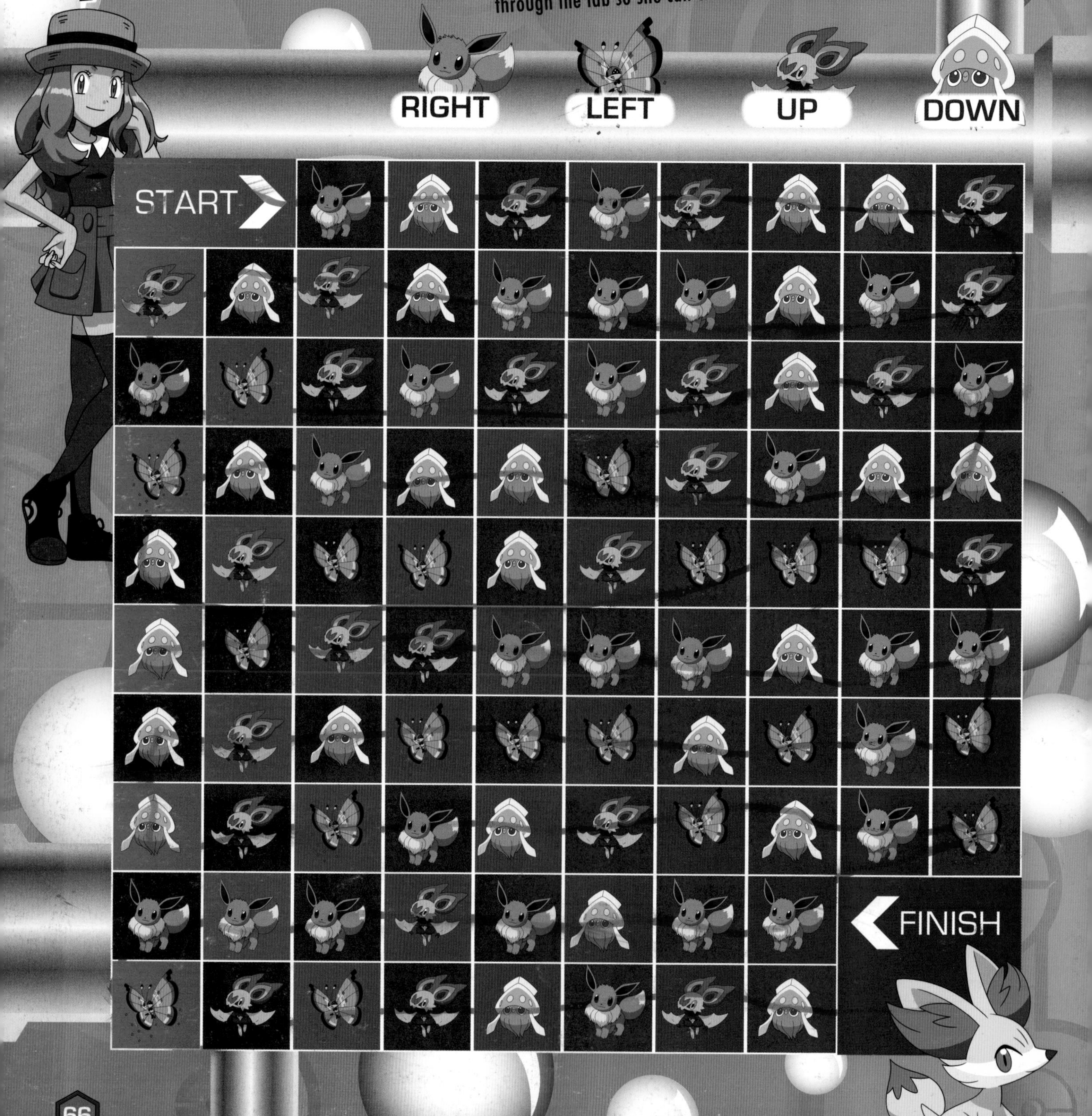

KALOS CONFUSION!

Ash has to make his way through the different terrains and cities of Kalos. Help him unscramble these place names so he can set out on his Pokémon journey.

ULOSIEM TYIC

....

REYCAMOS CHARSEER ALB

....

SRIMP WOTER

....

UNLEATSAN YICT

....

YESYODS GIVELLA

....

GLAYLEC IYTC

....

KALOS

CODEBREAKER

Ash needs to get a message to Clemont, but he's worried about it falling into the wrong hands. He's seen Team Rocket lurking around Lumiose City, so he's written the message in their secret Pokémon code. Use the alphabet code key below to decipher Ash's message.

A =
B =
C =
D = 

E = 
F = 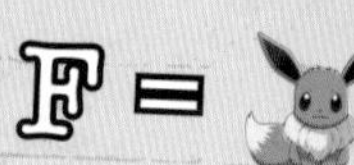
G = 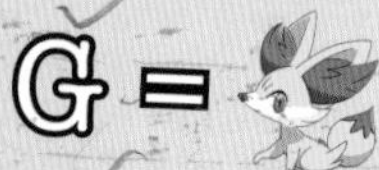
H = 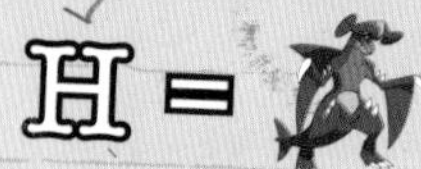

I =
J =
K =
L =

M =
N =
O =
P =

Q = 
R =
S =
T =

U = 
V =
W = 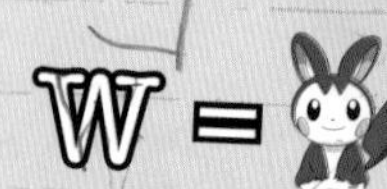

X =
Y =
Z =

ASH'S MESSAGE

Fantastic Furfrou-style!

GRAB SOME COLORED PENCILS AND GIVE THIS PRETTY FURFROU A FABULOUS NEW FUR-STYLE!

Furfrou love to be pampered and brushed. They can change their appearance by grooming; the more they are groomed, the more styles become available!

DID YOU KNOW? It's believed that in ancient times, Furfrou guarded the King of Kalos.

PROFESSOR SYCAMORE'S MISSING LINKS

Professor Sycamore has a research lab in Lumiose City. He is a prominent Pokémon researcher at the forefront of groundbreaking research on Pokémon Evolution. Ash and his friends are amazed by some of the Professor's startling theories about Pokémon.

Help Professor Sycamore by taking a look at these Pokémon Evolution chains. Write in the missing stage to complete each one. To give you a helping hand, the professor has provided a picture list of the missing Pokémon.

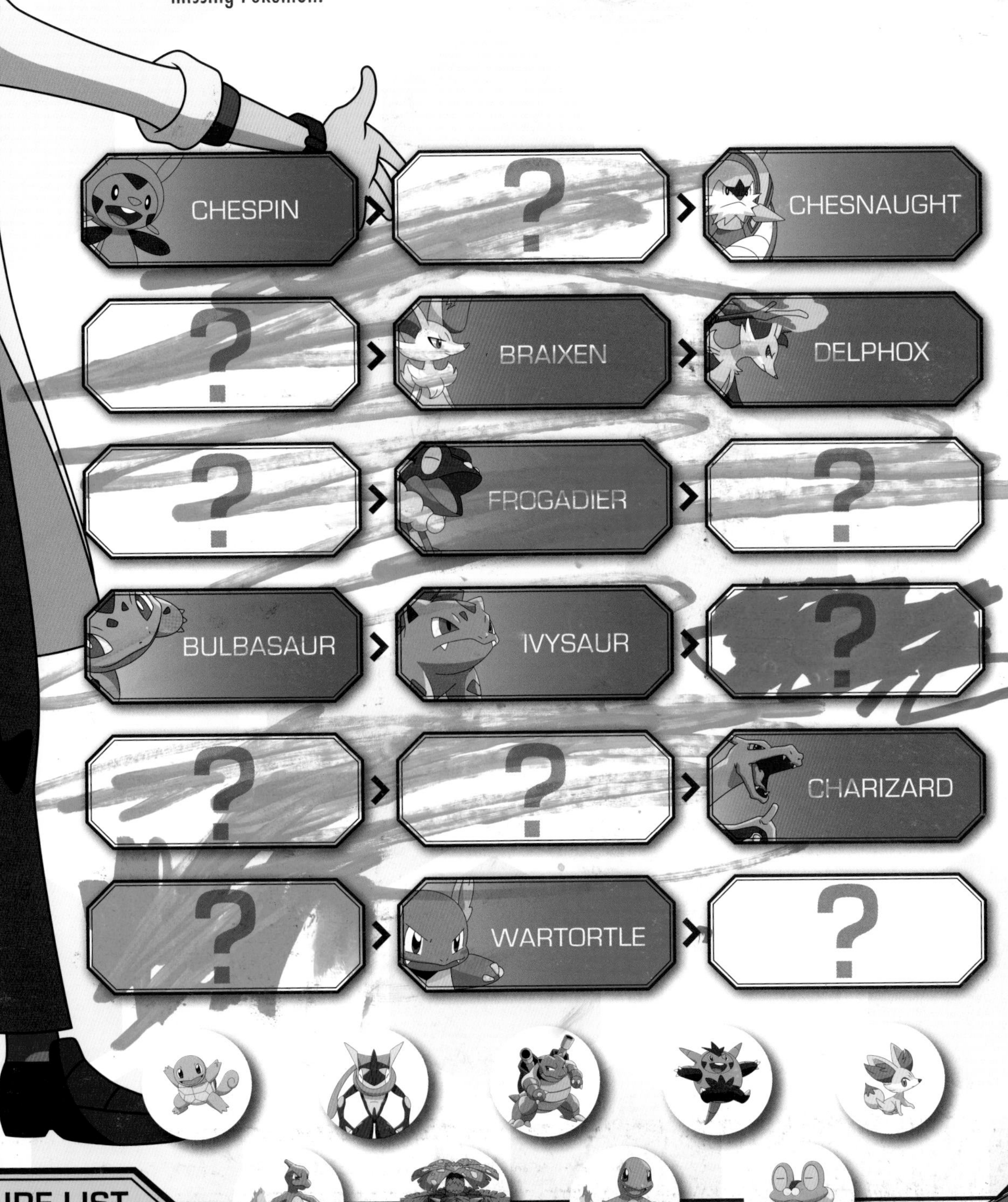

LEGENDARY KALOS DOOR HANGER!

No room is complete without this supercool Kalos door hanger! Trace, photocopy, or scan this template, stick it on cardboard, and then cut it out. Your door hanger is now ready to use.

ENTER

IF YOU DARE
FOR AN AWESOME
KALOS ADVENTURE!

DO NOT ENTER

AWESOME POKÉMON
GYM BATTLE
IN PROGRESS!

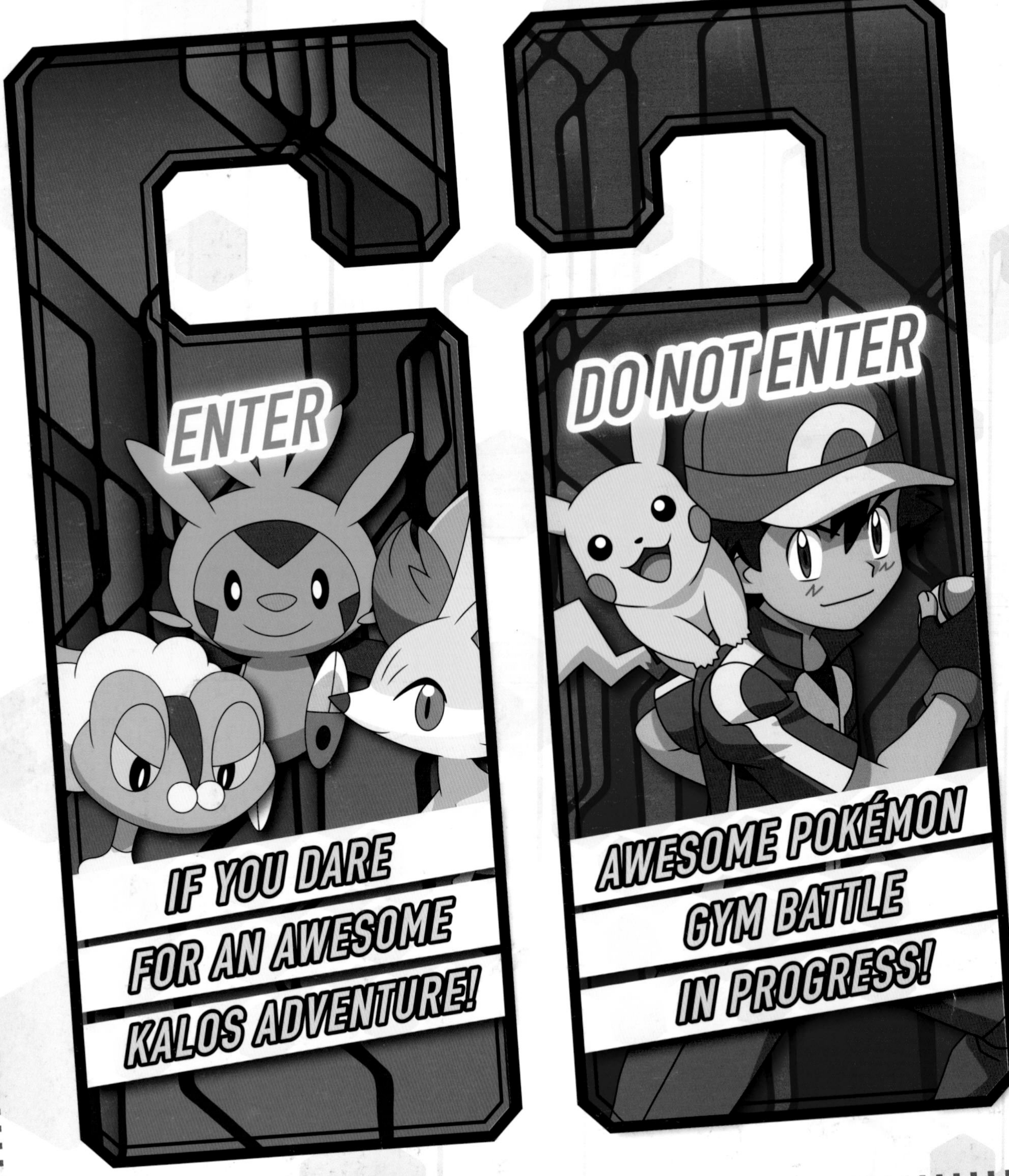

ANSWERS

KALOS CHALLANGE Pages 20-21

1. Central, Coastal, Mountain
2. Fletchling
3. 8 badges
4. Electric- and Fairy-type
5. Professor Sycamore
6. Prism Tower
7. Chespin, Fennekin, or Froakie
8. Xerneas, Yveltal, and Zygarde
9. Froakie
10. Rhyhorn racing

THE ROAD TO SANTALUNE Page 22

Dedenne
Electric- and Fairy-type

KALOS WORD SEARCH Page 23

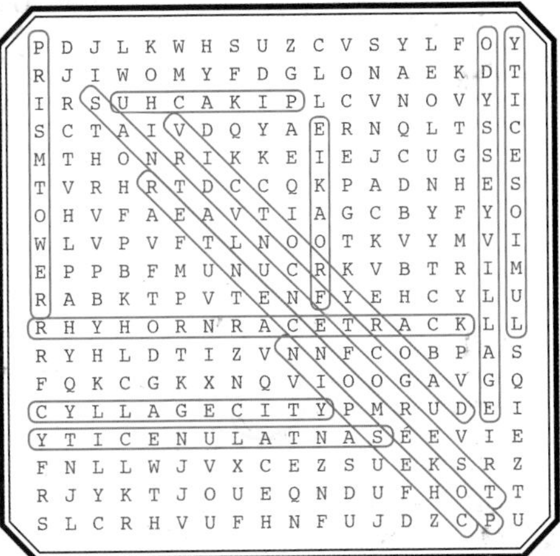

KALOS ADVENTURE CROSSWORD Page 32

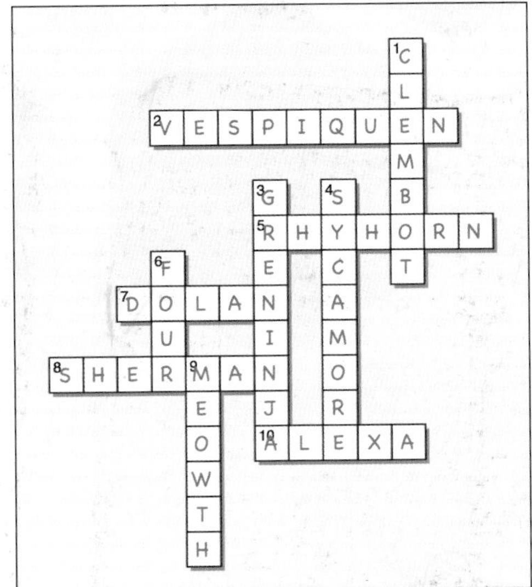

GOTTA CATCH 'EM ALL! Page 33

WHO'S WHO? Page 34

1. Blastoise
2. Jigglypuff
3. Marill
4. Charmander
5. Pancham
6. Quilladin
7. Furfrou
8. Scatterbug

POKÉMON TYPE TEST Page 35

1 Zoroark = Dark
2 Pumpkaboo = Ghost-Grass
3 Squirtle = Water
4 Litleo = Fire/Normal
5 Wigglytuff = Normal/Fairy
6 Gogoat = Grass
7 Croagunk = Poison-Fighting
8 Raichu = Electric
9 Glaceon = Ice
10 Wobbuffet = Psychic

BATTLE MOVE MATCH Page 44

Battle 1:
Pikachu Moves: Quick Attack, Iron Tail, Electro Ball, Thunderbolt
Surskit Moves: Ice Beam, Sticky Web, Protect

Battle 2
Fletchling Moves: Peck, Double Team, Razor Wind
Surskit Moves: Ice Beam, Sticky Web

Battle 3
Fletchling Moves: Peck
Vivillon Moves: Psychic, Gust, Sticky Web

SHADOW PLAY Page 47

1. Alakazam
2. Bulbasaur
3. Helioptile
4. Salamence
5. Talonflame
6. Vaporeon

KALOS POKÉMON PATTERNS Page 55

SERENA'S FIRST POKÉMON Page 66

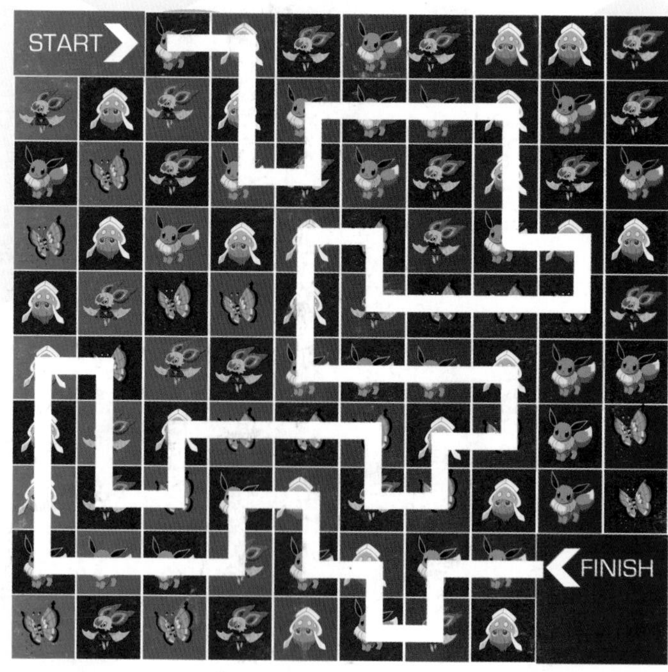

KALOS CONFUSION Page 67

1. LUMIOSE CITY
2. SYCAMORE RESEARCH LAB
3. PRISM TOWER
4. SANTALUNE CITY
5. ODYSSEY VILLAGE
6. CYLLAGE CITY

KALOS CODEBREAKER Page 69

Meet me by the fallen tree in the forest. I want to catch a Fairy-type Pokémon. Prof. Sycamore says we might get lucky and find a Sylveon!

PROFESSOR SYCAMORE'S MISSING LINKS Page 71

Chespin - Quilladin - Chesnaught
Fennekin - Braixen - Delphox
Froakie - Frogadier - Greninja
Bulbasaur - Ivysaur - Venusaur
Charmander - Charmeleon - Charizard
Squirtle - Wartortle - Blastoise